He Traced Her Perfect Coral Lips With His Tongue, Then Coaxed Her To Open For Him.

When he stroked her tongue with his, he could tell from her soft moan that she was as turned on as he was.

Unfortunately, sitting on a bale of straw in a stable had to be one of the least sensual places on earth. Cursing himself as nine kinds of a fool for starting something he couldn't finish, he groaned and reluctantly broke the kiss.

"I think it's about time we took that hot shower," he said, setting her on her feet.

"We?" she asked as he rose to take her hand in his and hurry her toward the stable doors.

He didn't even try to stop his wicked grin. "I've decided it's about time for the ranch to 'go green.' We'll save water by showering together."

Dear Reader,

When I was offered the opportunity to participate in the DYNASTIES: THE JARRODS miniseries, not only was I honored to be asked to write *Expecting the Rancher's Heir,* I was intrigued by the idea of a no-strings affair suddenly becoming a very serious dilemma. Then when I discovered it was set in the beautiful Rocky Mountains, my imagination took off.

Shortly after returning to Aspen for the reading of her father's will, Melissa Jarrod entered into a no-strings affair with local rancher Shane McDermott, one of the investors in Jarrod Ridge Resort. They've managed to keep it from her family and the other investors, but when their liaison takes an unexpected turn, it's just a matter of time before their secret comes to light.

I hope you enjoy reading *Expecting the Rancher's Heir* as much as I enjoyed writing it. I love hearing from my readers. Please feel free to e-mail me at Kathie@kathiedenosky.com or send snail mail to P.O. Box 2064, Herrin, IL 62948. And don't forget to stop by my Web site, www.kathiedenosky.com.

All the best,

Kathie

KATHIE DeNOSKY

EXPECTING THE RANCHER'S HEIR

Silhouette®

Desire

Published by Silhouette Books
America's Publisher of Contemporary Romance

Special thanks and acknowledgment to Kathie DeNosky for her contribution to the DYNASTIES: THE JARRODS miniseries.

This book is dedicated to the wonderful authors I worked with on this miniseries—Maureen Child, Maxine Sullivan, Tessa Radley, Emilie Rose and Heidi Betts. It was a pleasure working with all of you.

And a special thank-you to Charles Griemsman and Krista Stroever for asking me to be included in such a great project.

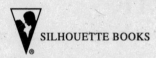 SILHOUETTE BOOKS

Recycling programs for this product may not exist in your area.

ISBN-13: 978-0-373-73049-0

EXPECTING THE RANCHER'S HEIR

Copyright © 2010 by Harlequin Books S.A.

Visit Silhouette Books at www.eHarlequin.com

Printed in U.S.A.

KATHIE DeNOSKY

lives in her native southern Illinois with her big, lovable Bernese mountain dog, Nemo. Highly sensual with a generous amount of humor, Kathie's books have appeared on the Waldenbooks bestseller list and received a Write Touch Readers' Award and a National Readers' Choice Award. Kathie enjoys going to rodeos, traveling to research settings for her books and listening to country music. Readers may contact Kathie at P.O. Box 2064, Herrin, Illinois 62948-5264 or e-mail her at kathie@kathiedenosky.com. They can also visit her Web site at www.kathiedenosky.com.

From the Last Will and Testament of Don Jarrod

....And to my daughter **Melissa,** I bequeath the third portion of my estate. In particular, I entrust you with executive oversight of the Jarrod Ridge spa complex. Though you may think I didn't notice, the success you've had with your fitness concern in Malibu truly impressed me. Ever since you were a little girl, I've been so proud of you, even though our family business kept me away from home, and from showing how much I truly loved you. I ask only that you make your younger half sister, Erica, feel as loved and welcome in her new family. You always held your own among your headstrong brothers; now show her the way.

One

"Don't say pregnant. Please don't say pregnant," Melissa Jarrod whispered, afraid to open her tightly closed eyes. Maybe if she repeated it enough times she could will the white stick in her trembling hand to give her the results she wanted.

When she finally worked up the courage to take a peek at the pregnancy test she held, her eyes widened and it felt as if her stomach dropped all the way to her feet. The word *pregnant* in the little results window couldn't have been clearer.

"I can't be pregnant," she said disbelievingly as she glanced at herself in the bathroom mirror. "We've been careful."

But as her gaze dropped to her flat stomach, she

realized that the way her luck had been running lately, it was not only possible, it was highly probable. She and Shane McDermott had been in a physical relationship practically from the moment she returned to Aspen two months ago. She sighed heavily. Although they'd taken the proper precautions, there had been that one night only a few days after they'd started seeing each other when they'd gotten carried away and passion had overtaken them.

Hoping the results of the test might be wrong, she quickly picked up the box to check the directions. No, she had done everything correctly. She turned the box to the side to see if there was a disclaimer or some reassurance that the test could have given a false-positive reading. Her spirits sank further when she found what she was looking for. The percentage of error was so low, it was almost impossible that she wasn't pregnant.

Wandering into the bedroom, she sank onto the side of the bed. What was she going to do and how on earth was she going to tell Shane?

He had made it perfectly clear from the beginning that he wasn't interested in a serious relationship, and that had been just fine with her. When she'd first come back to Aspen for the reading of her father's will, she hadn't been certain just how long she would be staying. But she, her brothers and her newfound half sister had learned they were required to take over the running of the Jarrod Ridge Resort for at least one year or forfeit their inheritance of the thriving enterprise. Even so, it would have been utter foolishness to engage in anything long-term, knowing that she would eventually return to California at some point in the future.

But with the positive results of the pregnancy test, their casual affair had just taken a very serious turn and become a lifelong commitment. At least for her. But how would Shane react when he learned that in a little more than seven months he was going to be a father?

Lost in a tangle of disturbing thoughts and fighting a wave of sheer panic, Melissa jumped when her cell phone rang. Reaching to pick it up from the nightstand, she noticed the number for the Tranquility Spa on the caller ID.

"What's wrong this time, Rita?" she asked, taking a deep steadying breath.

Whether real or imagined, the assistant manager of Jarrod Ridge's elite spa had reported a crisis nearly every day since Melissa had stepped in to temporarily take over the manager's position. But for the first time in two months, she welcomed the insecure woman's concerns. Anything was a welcome distraction from her own current dilemma.

"I'm sorry to bother you, Ms. Jarrod, but the yoga instructor called in sick this morning and I haven't been able to reach our backup. We have a room full of guests and no one to lead the yoga class. What should I do?" Rita whined, her voice clearly filled with indecision, as well as a good amount of panic.

"First of all, breathe, Rita," Melissa said, rising from the bed to pull a leotard from her dresser drawer. "I want you to calm down, then escort the guests over to the juice bar for a complimentary drink."

"Then what?" the woman asked, sounding a little more in control of herself.

How on earth the woman had managed to land the assistant-manager position, Melissa would never know. Although Rita was very nice, she couldn't make a decision on her own if her life depended on it.

Melissa checked her watch. "I'll be there in ten minutes to teach the class."

The last thing she wanted to do was lead a yoga session this morning. She needed to figure out when and how she was going to tell Shane, as well as her family, about the pregnancy. But the choice had been taken out of her hands. The Tranquility Spa had a stellar reputation for giving Jarrod Ridge guests five-star treatment and she wasn't about to let that status slip on her watch.

Putting her long blond hair into a ponytail, she stuffed her things into her gym bag, then grabbed her car keys from the kitchen counter as she started out the door of the lodge. Since her return to Aspen, she had been staying in Willow Lodge, one of the exclusive log cabins owned by Jarrod Ridge Resort.

She could have stayed in her suite at the family estate, but that had never been an option for her. Jarrod Manor might have been where she grew up, but she had always thought of it as more of a prison than she had a home. She hadn't been back but a handful of times since moving out to go to college eight years ago and she didn't particularly care to go back now.

As she steered her SUV under the canopy of the resort's main entrance, she relegated thoughts of her dismal, lonely childhood to the back of her mind. Even though Willow Lodge was the cabin farthest away from the manor, she could have walked the short distance. But as soon as the yoga class was over, she fully intended to make the drive over to the next valley where Shane's ranch was located and tell him there had been an unexpected complication in their no-strings relationship. That is if she could find the place.

She had only been to Rainbow Bend Ranch once and that had been years ago. If she remembered correctly it was in a remote valley that was several miles off the main road.

When she parked the Mountaineer, her heart raced at the sight of the man standing beside the truck just in front of hers. Shane McDermott was handing his keys to one of the valets and she didn't think she had ever seen him look so darned sexy.

Tall and devilishly handsome, he was a cowboy from the top of his wide-brimmed black Resistol to the soles of his big-booted feet. Shane was the type of man she had always fantasized about, and if the expressions on the faces of the female guests standing by the resort's main entrance were any indication, he was the type of man they dreamed about, too.

No wonder he had a reputation for being a ladies' man. They were drawn to him like bees to pollen.

Her heart came to a complete halt when he walked over to open the driver's door of her SUV.

"Good morning, Ms. Jarrod," he said, removing his hat as any self-respecting cowboy would do when greeting a lady.

A slight breeze ruffled his thick black hair and it reminded her of how it had looked the other night after she had run her fingers through it when they'd made love. She did her best to ignore the tingle that coursed through her at the thought of what they had shared.

"Good morning, Mr. McDermott," she answered, getting out of the car to hand her keys to one of the uniformed valets.

"I thought Friday was your day off," he said, smiling congenially.

"It usually is." She breezed past him and hurried toward the resort doors. "One of the spa's yoga instructors called in sick this morning and I'm going to have to teach her class."

He fell into step beside her. "After you finish twisting the resort's guests into pretzels do you have the rest of the day off?"

"Yes."

She couldn't help but wonder where Shane was going with his line of questioning. In order to avoid gossip among the Jarrod Ridge employees and the disapproval of some of the older, less progressive-minded investors, they'd been extremely careful to conceal their affair. Not even her family knew about them, and they had managed to maintain the appearance of being nothing more than acquaintances by limiting being seen together. They hadn't even spent an entire night together for fear of someone seeing him leave her place. Thus far, they'd been successful by not being seen together at all.

But if Shane continued questioning her as they walked toward the spa, there was a very real possibility that someone would take notice, and by the end of the day, the rumors about them would be spread all over the resort, if not the entire town of Aspen. Or even worse, her nerves could very well get the better of her and she would blurt out in the middle of the crowded lobby that she going to have his baby.

Neither scenario was appealing. She knew for certain that she couldn't cope with the fallout that was sure to follow on top of everything else she had to deal with.

"I'll come by Willow Lodge later," he said, smiling. His icy blue eyes danced with mischief. "I have something I want to talk to you about, Lissa."

"Would you keep your voice down?" she hissed.

She quickly looked around to see if anyone overheard him. He was the only person who had ever called her Lissa and it never failed to send an exciting little thrill coursing through her.

"I have something I need to discuss with you, too, Shane. But I'd rather not go into it…" Her voice trailed off when a bellman seemed to take more than a passing interest in seeing them together. When the man moved on, she turned back to Shane. "I thought you were supposed to have a luncheon meeting today with some of the other Jarrod Ridge investors, Mr. McDermott."

"I do." He looked as if he didn't have a care in the world, and she couldn't help but wonder how quickly that would change when she shared her news.

"Then what are you doing here now?"

Melissa hadn't meant to sound so blunt, but if she didn't get to the yoga class pretty soon, poor Rita was sure to suffer a nervous breakdown and guests would start complaining. Besides, she needed to put some space between herself and Shane. The scent of leather and woodsy aftershave were playing havoc with her equilibrium and it was all she could do to keep from swaying toward him.

"I came early to see that the new herd of trail horses I sold the resort is living up to expectation." He arched one dark eyebrow. "Do you have a problem with that?"

Sighing, Melissa shook her head. "I'm sorry, I didn't mean to be so short with you. The yoga class was supposed to start fifteen minutes ago and I really do need to get to the spa."

"Then I won't keep you, Ms. Jarrod." His voice grew a bit louder as they reached the entrance to Tranquility Spa and she knew it was for the benefit of anyone who might be eavesdropping. He gave her a conspiratorial wink as he dipped his head ever so slightly and touched the wide brim of his cowboy hat. "It was nice running into you again. I hope you have a nice Labor Day weekend."

As she watched Shane turn and stroll down the hall toward the meeting rooms, Melissa sighed. The man looked almost as good from the back as he did from the front. His Western-cut, dark brown suit jacket emphasized the width of his strong shoulders and his blue jeans fit his long, muscular legs to perfection.

His well-toned physique rivaled that of a Greek god and she had intimate knowledge of the power and strength of each and every muscle when he had held her, kissed her, made love to her.

A tiny shiver streaked straight up her spine. She forced herself to ignore the sudden warmth that followed as it spread throughout her body. Opening the door to the spa, she took a deep breath and prepared to teach the yoga class.

Lusting after Shane McDermott was what had landed her in her current predicament. It would definitely be in her best interests to remember that.

"Melissa, did you hear me?" Avery Lancaster asked. Engaged to Melissa's brother Guy, the petite blonde had become a very close friend in the month since they met.

"Um, sorry," Melissa murmured as she took a sip of her water. With her mind still reeling from the results of the pregnancy test, she found it hard to concentrate on the conversation.

"I asked if you've tried the cucumber sandwiches Guy added?" her friend asked patiently as she pointed to the leather-bound folder Melissa held.

Perusing the new healthy-choices section her brother had added to the Sky Lounge lunch menu since taking over managing the resort's restaurants, Melissa shook her head. "No, I hadn't even noticed the new dishes."

Avery frowned. "Is something wrong?"

"Oh, just the usual stuff that goes along with managing a spa," Melissa lied, closing the menu and setting it on the table. She hated not being truthful with her friend, but she needed to talk to Shane about the pregnancy before anyone else.

"Still having problems with your assistant manager, little sister?" Guy asked, walking over to join them. He leaned down to kiss Avery, then seated himself beside her.

"Actually, Rita is doing a little better than she was," Melissa said, thankful to have something to focus on besides her own dilemma. "She did have a moment this morning when I thought her nerves were going to send her into a panic attack, but we got it straightened out."

"In other words, you took care of it," Guy said, knowingly.

"Well, yes," Melissa admitted. "But in all fairness to Rita, there wasn't anyone else to teach the yoga class this morning."

"Are you still taking the weekend off like you planned?" Avery asked.

"Blake thinks I should," Melissa said, shrugging. Guy's fraternal twin and the new CEO of Jarrod Ridge Resort, her oldest brother had pointed out at the last managers' meeting that she needed to back off to see if Rita could handle the assistant manager's position or if she needed to be replaced. "I'll only be a phone call away, so I don't suppose it would hurt to be off for a few days."

"You haven't taken any time for yourself since you started managing the spa," Guy pointed out. "We both know if Rita knows you're available, she'll call."

Melissa rubbed at the tension building at her temples. "I can't just leave her on her own. What if something happens like this morning?"

Guy looked thoughtful for a moment. "If Rita runs into something she can't handle, she can get hold of me or Blake. I'll be around most of the weekend, and you know that Blake will be, too."

"You and Blake both intimidate Rita." Melissa couldn't help but laugh. "Besides, what do you know about running a spa or teaching yoga?"

"Me? Intimidate someone?" Guy grinned. "Just

because I demand the best from my kitchen staff, it doesn't mean that I'm a tyrant." Reaching out, he patted her shoulder. "Don't worry. I'll take care of whatever comes up at the spa. You just relax and enjoy a little down time."

Never having been encouraged by their father to develop close family ties while they were growing up, Melissa and her four brothers had become a lot closer as adults. She couldn't help but wonder what it would have been like if they'd had a strong bond when they were children. Maybe growing up in Jarrod Manor wouldn't have been as lonely for her.

"Thanks, Guy," Melissa said, smiling. "If you need me…"

Her brother shook his head. "I won't." Checking his watch, he rose. "Break's over. Time to go back to the kitchen and see how things are going." He kissed Avery's cheek. "I'll see you this evening."

Watching Guy make his way across the crowded restaurant, Avery sighed happily. "Isn't he just the best-looking man ever?"

"You're in love," Melissa said, unable to keep from feeling a bit envious.

Although they'd had a rocky start, Avery and Guy had the kind of loving relationship she had always envisioned for herself. Unfortunately, what she and Shane had together would never go any further than what it was now—a strong physical attraction that would most likely cool considerably once he learned of her pregnancy.

As she and Avery finished lunch, they chatted about the upcoming dinner honoring the Food and Wine Gala investors. By the time they parted in the lobby an hour later, Melissa was more than ready to get back to Willow Lodge. Shane would be coming over soon, and although she had no idea how he would take the news about the baby, they needed to get used to the idea that in about seven months they were going to be parents.

Shane walked out of the meeting room toward the Jarrod Ridge lobby with a single-minded purpose—find Lissa and convince her to spend the three-day weekend with him at his ranch. The resort's annual Food and Wine Gala had been in full swing for the past couple of weeks, and everything had been extremely busy. The time they'd been able to spend together had been limited, and, now that the event was over, he fully intended to remedy that as soon as possible. He certainly wasn't looking for anything long-term to develop out of their affair, but he wasn't yet ready to give up on whatever they had going on between them, either. He had enjoyed spending time with her the past couple of months and looked forward to at least a couple more before they went their separate ways.

"Shane, my boy, it's good to see you again," a deep, booming voice said from somewhere behind him.

Stopping, Shane turned to smile at one of his

late father's oldest friends. "It's good to see you, too, Senator Kurk. How have you been?" he asked, shaking the man's hand.

"Can't complain," the senator said, smiling. Tall and commanding, the white-haired man had been a member of congress for as long as Shane could remember. "It's always good to get out of Washington for a few days and come back home to spend a little down time with my friends and family."

"I'm sure it is," Shane agreed. "I've heard they're keeping you busy these days with several important national issues."

Senator Kurk chuckled. "And if that isn't enough to keep me awake at night, I've been named the head of a new investigative committee." He looked thoughtful. "Aren't you an architect?"

Shane nodded. "I specialize in stables."

"Interesting," the man said. "I suppose your studies included other areas of architecture, as well?"

"Of course." When the man remained silent, Shane started inching away. "I'm sure you'll get to the bottom of whatever it is your committee is looking into, Senator," he said, hoping the man wasn't at liberty to share what the committee was investigating.

As much as he liked Patrick Kurk, the good senator could be as long-winded and boring as any other politician, and Shane had plans that didn't include listening to him drone on about what ailed the nation. The sooner he got over to the lodge, the sooner he would start what he was certain would be a very enjoyable weekend with one of the most exciting women he had ever had the pleasure of knowing.

"Excuse me, Senator," one of the man's aides said, hurrying up to join them. "The Rotary Club meeting is about to begin and your speech is first on the agenda, right after the opening remarks."

Relieved that his trip over to Willow Lodge wouldn't be delayed any further, Shane smiled. "I won't keep you, Senator. Maybe we can get together for some trout fishing on the Rainbow River the next time you're in town."

"I'll take you up on that the first chance I get," Senator Kurk said, turning to go. "It was good seeing you again, Shane."

Walking out of the resort, Shane forgot all about politicians and senatorial committees as he started out. He was on a mission to get Lissa to join him for the three-day weekend and he wasn't going to give up until he got what he wanted.

Given her concerns about feeding the gossip mongers at the resort, he was pretty sure it wouldn't be all that easy to talk her into staying with him at Rainbow Bend. But there wasn't a doubt in his mind that what they shared would be worth whatever he had to do to convince her.

Shane shook his head as he looked around to see if anyone was watching, then took the hidden shortcut back toward the luxury lodges. He had been jumping through hoops for the past couple of months just to please her, and it was beginning to get old.

Instead of going directly to the lodge where she was staying, it had become a ritual for him to head toward the stables, then cut back through a small patch of woods. She had insisted that no one would think anything of him going to check on the herd of horses he had sold the resort, and he supposed she was right. But he couldn't control other people's opinions of him and didn't give a damn what they thought anyway. Lissa, on the other hand, was a very private person and he respected her need for discretion even if he didn't completely understand it.

Slipping through the stand of pine trees behind Willow Lodge, he took the porch steps two at a time. Just as he raised his hand to knock, Lissa opened the door.

"What took you so long?" she asked, taking him by the hand to pull him inside.

As soon as they cleared the doorway, he took her into his arms and used his boot to shove the door shut behind them. "I don't know a man alive who doesn't want to hear a woman ask that question, angel."

She looked as if she had something more on her mind, but it would just have to wait. It had been almost three days since he had held her, kissed her, and he had every intention of immediately remedying that particular problem.

His mouth came down on hers, and she let out a

startled little squeak, but to his satisfaction, she didn't protest or try to push him away. Instead, she wrapped her arms around his waist and pressed herself against him.

Her response to him never failed to send a flash fire rushing from the top of his head straight to the region south of his belt buckle. Today was no different. In the blink of an eye, he was hotter than a two-dollar pistol on a Saturday night.

Shifting to pull her more fully into him, Shane deepened the kiss. As he stroked and teased, her sweet taste, the floral scent of her silky blond hair and the feel of her soft body pressed to his much harder one had him feeling as if his jeans had shrunk at least two sizes in the stride. He quickly decided that he would do well to end the kiss or there was a good chance he'd end up emasculating himself.

"I've been wanting to do that ever since I saw you at the resort this morning," he said, leaning back to smile down at her.

The dazed look in her vibrant blue eyes and the heat of passion coloring her creamy cheeks was one of the most beautiful sights he had ever been privileged to see. Soft and feminine, Lissa looked the way a woman was meant to look when a man kissed her.

She shook her head as if to clear it. "Shane, before this goes any further. We need to talk."

"Yes, we do," he agreed.

"There's something I need to tell you."

"Me first," he insisted.

He took her by the hand and led her into the great room. Settling himself into one of the oversize leather chairs in front of the stone fireplace, he pulled her down to sit on his lap.

"This is really important, Shane. There's been an unexpected development that—"

He placed his index finger to her soft lips. "It'll have to wait."

"This is something that can't wait."

He gave her a quick kiss to divert her. "I have something I want you to do with me this weekend."

The kiss distracted her just as he had intended. "W-what?"

"I want you to spend the next few days at my ranch with me." When it looked as if she was about to protest, he shook his head. "Hear me out, angel. Most of my ranch hands are off for the holiday weekend and the ones who aren't couldn't care less who I have staying with me. Cactus, my housekeeper, has already left to visit his sister in Denver for the next few days, and we'll have the entire house to ourselves. Unless you tell them, no one who cares will ever be the wiser that you stayed with me."

She looked thoughtful for several long moments before she finally nodded. "We need to discuss something at length and I think it would be a very good idea to have the privacy of your ranch to do it."

Surprised and more than a little pleased by how easily she had agreed, he hugged her close. "Talking wasn't what I had in mind when I asked you to go with me. But I guess we can hash over whatever you think is so important while we rest up from more pleasurable pursuits."

She gave him a warning look. "Will you be serious?"

"Angel, I thought you'd have figured out by now that when it comes to making love, I'm always serious," he murmured as he kissed the side of her slender neck. "But if you think it's necessary, I'll be more than happy to take a few minutes to refresh your memory."

"After I tell you what I discovered this morning, I think you'll agree that there should be less emphasis on teasing and making love this weekend and more concentration on making some very serious decisions about what we're going to do," she said, pulling from his arms to stand up. He watched her shoulders rise and fall as she took several deep breaths. "Shane, there's no easy way to put this and I doubt you'll be happy to hear about it."

His smile slowly faded. Her body language and the seriousness of her tone warned him that whatever was on her mind was most likely something unpleasant. But he had never been one to avoid an obvious problem. He preferred to hit the difficulty head-on, deal with it and move forward.

"Why don't you just tell me outright and get it over with, Lissa?"

"A-all right."

The slight tremor in her voice and the lone tear slowly slipping down her cheek when she turned to face him caused his heart to stutter and had him moving to get to his feet in the blink of an eye. But her next words stopped him stone cold.

"Shane, I'm…pregnant."

Two

Feeling as if he had taken a sucker punch to the gut, Shane stared at her as he sank back down into the plush chair. Rarely at a loss for words, he suddenly couldn't have strung two words together if his life depended on it.

Pregnant. Lissa was pregnant. That meant he was going to be a…he swallowed hard against the knot forming in his stomach…a daddy.

Un-freaking-believable.

He shook his head in an effort to make some sense of his tangled thoughts. He wasn't sure what he had expected her to tell him, but the fact that she was having a baby—his baby—certainly hadn't been it.

Hell, he had never expected any woman to announce that he had made her pregnant.

"The baby belongs to you," Lissa said, sounding a little defensive.

He shook his head. "There wasn't a doubt in my mind about that, angel. When did you see the doctor?"

"I haven't." She bit her lower lip to keep it from trembling and he knew she was thoroughly stressed. "I just took the home test this morning."

"Maybe it was wrong."

"I don't think so. I've missed one period and getting close to missing the second." Her shoulders slumped. "Besides, the test boasts the highest accuracy rate of all the in-home brands."

Suddenly needing a good dose of fresh air and a little time to come to grips with her news, Shane rose to his feet. Walking over to her, he used the pad of his thumb to wipe the tear from her cheek.

"Why don't you pack a bag for the weekend while I go get my truck?"

"But what if someone sees us leaving town together?" she asked, looking uncertain.

"We've got bigger things to worry about than what some busybody with nothing better to do than spread gossip is going to say about seeing the two of us together," he interrupted, anticipating her argument. Taking her into his arms, he pressed a quick kiss to her forehead. "Once we get to Rainbow Bend, we can discuss things, sort it all out and decide what we're going to do. For now, get your things together and be ready to go when I get back." Without waiting for her to change her mind or find an excuse to stay at the resort, he quickly released her and walked outside.

Pulling the door closed behind him, Shane stood on the deck for several mind-numbing moments and gazed at the panoramic view of the Rocky Mountains against the bright blue September sky. Splashes of gold from the aspen trees making their annual autumn transformation painted the slopes and quavered delicately in the slight breeze. He saw none of it.

He was too focused on the fact that he had done the one thing he had sworn he would never do. Hell, he had never even considered fathering a child as part of his life plan.

But he had just learned that particular horse had left the barn and there was no sense in closing the gate now. As he saw it, all there was left to do was man up, accept his responsibilities and do the right thing. It was what his morals demanded and his father would have expected of him.

Filling his lungs with the crisp mountain air, Shane straightened his shoulders and descended the steps. Walking toward the main part of the resort, he knew exactly what he had to do.

He had made Melissa Jarrod pregnant. Now, it was time for him to make her his wife.

The drive to Shane's ranch was mostly spent in quiet reflection as they both contemplated the ramifications of the unexpected turn in their no-strings affair. By the time they reached Rainbow Valley, Melissa felt as if her nerves were stretched to the breaking point. Grappling for something—anything—to keep from thinking about their dilemma, she glanced around.

She had only been to the Rainbow Bend Ranch once before and that had been several years ago when her father had coerced her into accompanying him on a horse-buying trip for the resort. It had been a lame attempt on his part to bridge the ever-widening gap between them. She hadn't wanted to be there and spent the time wishing she was anywhere else, instead of taking in the gorgeous scenery.

But as Shane drove the truck over the ridge and down the winding road leading into the picturesque valley, she couldn't get over the breathtaking view. "This is beautiful, Shane. You're so lucky that you got to grow up here."

"I like it," he said, stopping the truck beside a rustic two-story log ranch house. "But not everyone appreciates the isolation."

Melissa frowned. "You make it sound as if it's stuck out in the middle of nowhere. I wouldn't consider ten miles outside of Aspen all that far from civilization."

"That's because you haven't been here in the winter," he answered, shrugging one shoulder. "When we get a heavy snow, the road up on the ridge can be closed off for weeks at a time, making trips into town few and far between."

"How did you get back and forth to go to school when you were a child?" she asked, remembering that he had graduated with honors.

"When I was younger and winter hit, I stayed in Aspen with my dad's sister and her family until they moved to New Mexico." He got out of the truck and walked around to open the passenger door for her. "By the time they left Colorado, I was almost out of school and old enough to stay on my own."

"That's when you stayed at Jarrod Ridge, wasn't it?" she guessed. Required by her father to work at the resort after school and on weekends, she vaguely remembered seeing Shane working with the horses the few times she had escorted guests to the stables.

Nodding, he reached into the bed of the truck for her overnight case, then placed his hand on the small of her back as he guided her toward the house. "My dad and yours had an agreement that I could stay at Jarrod Ridge the winter of my senior year, in exchange for me wrangling on the weekends and acting as a guide on some of the trail rides."

"Considering how much you've always loved horses, you probably didn't have much of a problem with that," she said, smiling as they climbed the steps to the wraparound porch.

He shook his head, then reached around her to open the front door. "Since the resort buys all of its stock exclusively from Rainbow Bend, it was like taking care of my own horses."

When they entered the house, Melissa got her first glimpse of Shane's home and it came as no surprise that everything from the pieces of antique harness and tack decorating the walls to the foyer's chandelier made of elk antlers was rugged and thoroughly masculine. Just like the owner. There wasn't so much as a hint that a woman had ever lived there and she couldn't help but wonder what had happened to his mother.

Melissa tried to think if she had heard anything about the woman. Nothing came to mind. Had his mother passed away when Shane was a child like her mother had?

"Cactus left this morning for Denver, so we'll be on our own for meals," Shane said, interrupting her thoughts. He hung his wide-brimmed hat on a peg beside the door, set her small bag on the floor and reached to help her out of her jacket. "Just let me know when you get hungry and I'll throw a couple of steaks on the grill."

She frowned. "For the past couple of weeks, it seems that I'm hungry all of the time."

"Is that because of the pregnancy?" She watched his gaze zero in on her midsection as if he was looking for a significant change to have taken place in the past few days. Apparently finding none, he raised his gaze to meet hers. "I remember one of my hired men joking about his wife eating like a field hand when she was pregnant with their little boy."

"I wouldn't say I'm that bad yet, but I do think the pregnancy could be the cause for the increase in my appetite." She nibbled on her lower lip as she tried to remember what some of her friends had mentioned about the early stages of their pregnancies. Nothing came to mind about constantly being hungry. "Since I've never been pregnant before, I'm not really sure," she said, shrugging.

He stared at her for several long seconds before nodding. "We'll have to check with your doctor about that when you go for your first visit." Looking thoughtful, he added, "In fact, it would probably be a good idea to start making a list of the things we need to ask him."

"Whoa, there, Cowboy. What do you mean by 'we'?" She shook her head. "I don't remember inviting you to go along with me."

"Doesn't matter. I'm going," he stated, as if it were a foregone conclusion.

"Why?"

"We'll discuss my reasoning later, as well as make a few important decisions," he said, giving her the same charming grin that never failed to make her pulse race. He picked up her bag and ushered her toward the stairs. "Right now, I'll show you to the bedroom and let you freshen up while I put the steaks on to cook."

When he guided her up the steps and down the

hall, she was a bit surprised that he opened a door and showed her into one of the guest rooms. They'd never spent an entire night together and she had assumed when he asked her to spend the weekend with him, he had intended for her to sleep in his room. But after hearing the news of her pregnancy, she had no doubt that his previous insatiable desire for her had cooled considerably.

He set her bag on the bed, then turning to go, took her into his arms. "When you get ready, come down to the kitchen. I should have supper ready in about twenty minutes." Then, before she could react, he softly kissed her cheek and left the room.

As she unzipped her case and started to put her clothes away, a sadness she couldn't quite understand filled her. Why did Shane's diminishing interest in her bother her so much?

It wasn't as if they were in love. They had both agreed before beginning their affair that the time they spent together would be relaxed and casual with no emotional involvement getting in the way of their respective careers.

Now that she had been given the responsibilities of running the resort's world-class spa, she had her hands full. She would love to have a husband and family of her own one day, but now just wasn't a good time to do it. Besides, Shane wasn't the right man to make that dream come true. His reputation for moving from one woman to another was only slightly better than her brother Trevor's.

Along with raising championship quarter horses, Shane was a highly successful architect specializing in the design of exclusive stables. His client list included some of the richest, most famous people in the equine world and he simply didn't have time for more than a casual relationship, anyway.

Melissa bit her lower lip to keep it from trembling. It was times like this that she missed having a mother the most. She would love to be able to turn to her mother and ask for her advice. Unfortunately, Margaret Jarrod had died of cancer when Melissa was two and she had grown up without the love and nurturing guidance of a mother.

Shaking off her uncharacteristic gloominess, she finished unpacking, then took a deep breath and stepped out into the hallway as she headed for the stairs. She had known her time with Shane would end at some point. She just hadn't realized it would be so soon. Nor could she have anticipated that she would be pregnant with his baby when it happened.

"When do you intend to call the doctor's office for your first appointment?" Shane asked, reaching for his glass of iced tea. Lissa had been extremely quiet for most of the meal and it was past time they addressed the issue that had been on both of their minds since she made her announcement that afternoon.

When she looked up from the bite of steak she had been pushing around the plate with her fork, she shook her head. "I really haven't thought that far ahead. I only took the test this morning. Then, before I had the chance to recover from the shock of the results, I was called to take over the yoga class at the spa and later met Avery for lunch."

"Shortly after you finished that, I showed up at your door and here we are," he guessed.

She nodded. "I still haven't had time to fully comprehend the fact that I'm actually going to have a baby."

"It is pretty unreal, isn't it?" He was having a hard time wrapping his mind around that fact himself.

Her vivid blue gaze reflected some barely contained panic and he was fairly certain he had that deer-in-the-headlights look about him, as well.

"I knew it was possible," she said, finally laying her fork down. "But seriously, only one time unprotected and I get pregnant? The odds against that happening have to be pretty high."

"Looks like that's all it took for us." He reached across the table to cover her hand with his. "But I want you to know, you aren't going to have to go through this alone. We're in this together. I'll be there to support you every step of the way, Lissa."

"I appreciate that." She stared at him for several long moments before she finally sat back from the table. "But if you mean monetarily, I think we both know that isn't necessary. I'm financially independent and have more than enough to handle whatever expenses there are before and after the birth."

Given their initial agreement to keep things casual, he could understand her misinterpretation of his promise, as well as her reluctance to believe he would commit himself to anything more than monetary assistance. But the idea that she considered him so shallow and irresponsible that he would just walk away from her and the child they created still didn't sit well.

"I'm not talking about child support," he stated, doing his best to keep his tone even.

"What *are* you talking about, Shane?" she asked, looking confused.

Rising to place their plates on the kitchen counter, he turned to face her. "I'm telling you that I'll be with you for doctor appointments, the baby's birth and raising him."

"In other words, you're telling me you're going to want joint custody." She nodded. "I can understand that and I don't see a problem. I'm sure we can work something out."

"Custody is going to be a nonissue," he said, shaking his head. He walked over to squat down beside her chair, then reaching up to brush a strand of long blond hair from her cheek, he smiled. "I'm pretty sure that sharing the responsibility of a child is automatic when his parents are married."

Her eyes widened and her mouth opened and closed several times as she obviously tried to find her voice. "Married?" she finally gasped.

"Yes."

Her expression stated louder than words ever could that she didn't believe him. "*Married* as in the tiered cake, white dress and 'I do'?"

"Yup."

"No."

"Why not?"

She closed her eyes, then opening them, shook her head as she pinned him with her crystalline gaze. "Have you lost your mind, Shane? You can't possibly be serious."

"Angel, marriage is one subject I never joke about," he said, meaning it.

"We can't get married, Shane," she insisted. "Beyond the basics, we really don't know that much about each other."

"Sure we do." He stood up and, lifting her into his arms, sat down in the chair to settle her on his lap. "I know you like when I do this." Kissing the side of her neck, he was rewarded with her soft sigh. "And you really like this," he added, slipping his hand beneath the tail of her aqua T-shirt. He used his fingertip to trace the satiny skin covering her ribs. As he slowly lowered his head, he moved his hand. "But you love this."

His mouth covered hers at the same time his hand cupped her breast and to his immense satisfaction, Lissa didn't so much as put up a token protest. Encouraged by her response, Shane deepened the kiss and once again marveled at her sweetness and the feeling of completion he always experienced when he held her.

He had kissed a lot of women in his time, but not one of them made him feel the way Melissa Jarrod did. Her slender body fit perfectly against his and her passion never failed to excite him in ways he could have never imagined.

His lower body tightened predictably and he decided he had better break the kiss before things got out of hand. At the moment, Lissa needed his comfort far more than she did his lust.

Drawing in some much-needed air, he smiled. "I told you I knew a lot about you."

She shook her head as if to clear it. "I wasn't talking about pleasing each other sexually and you know it."

"Correct me if I'm wrong, but isn't that a huge part of marriage?" he asked, unable to keep from grinning.

"Maybe for a man, but a woman needs more from a relationship than just good sex," she insisted. "*I* need more."

He raised one eyebrow. "Would you care to enlighten me?"

Leaning back, she stared at him for a moment as if she thought he might be a little on the simple side. "Do you realize we've never spent more than a few hours together at any one time? I may know you intimately in bed, but I don't know anything about you otherwise. I don't know what you like to read, what kind of movies you prefer or even what your favorite color is."

He frowned. "I don't see how any of that would make or break a marriage."

She pulled from his arms and stood up. "Don't you see? Those are the kinds of things you know about the person you are committing to spend the rest of your life with." Sighing heavily, she turned to face him. "I don't even know what side of the bed you sleep on or if you snore."

"So you're telling me that knowing whether I snore or not is more important than a gratifying love life?" he asked, laughing.

If looks could kill, the one she sent his way would have him laid out in two shakes of a squirrel's tail. "Will you be serious, Shane? I'm trying to explain what constitutes a committed relationship."

Oh, he knew exactly what she was driving at. Lissa thought she needed to know what made him tick. But she was wanting more from him than he was comfortable giving. He had never been in the habit of sharing more than the surface details about himself with anyone and he wasn't inclined to do so now.

Unfortunately, if he wanted her to go along with his plan, he was going to have to give her something she considered relevant. "Nonfiction, action-adventure, red and left."

She looked confused.

"I mainly read nonfiction and my favorite movies are action-adventure. I like the color red and I prefer the middle of the bed. But if I had to choose a side, it would be the left." He grinned. "As for the snoring, you can let me know about that tomorrow morning."

"Those things are nice to know," she said, looking a little more satisfied with his answers. "But that's just the tip of the iceberg."

Before she could press him further and delve into areas he would rather not go into, he decided to turn the tables and ask a few questions of his own. "What about you? What is there about Lissa Jarrod that you think I need to know?"

He gave himself a mental pat on the back at her pleased expression. "Let's see. I like pizza, I hate Brussels sprouts—"

"Who doesn't?" he said, making a face.

She laughed. "And I adore romantic movies."

"What about horses?" he asked, wondering if they had that in common. "Do you like to ride?"

"I haven't ridden in several years, but I used to enjoy going on some of the trail rides offered at Jarrod Ridge." Smiling, she added, "I even had a favorite horse named Smoky Joe that I always rode."

Shane stood up and took her into his arms. "I don't remember you going on any of the rides I guided."

Loosely wrapping her arms around his waist, she gazed up at him. "That was because I was too young. When you were eighteen and leading those trail rides, I was only eleven."

"Now hold on just a minute," he said, frowning.

"Didn't you tell me one time that you worked at the resort when I did?"

"Yes." He felt her body tense. "Of course, I wasn't on the payroll. But I started doing simple things like delivering messages from one office to another. That was when I was eight."

"Ah, the pre-e-mail and text-messaging days."

She nodded. "By the time I turned ten I had graduated to showing guests how to find their way around the resort grounds. Then, at sixteen, I started working the front desk."

Shane wasn't opposed to a kid doing a few chores. Hell, his dad had him mucking out stalls and feeding horses from the time he was old enough to carry a feed bucket. But it sounded as if Donald Jarrod had his kids doing more than just simple chores.

"Whose idea was it for you to go to work at such an early age?" he asked, remembering that he had seen all of the Jarrod children working various jobs around the resort.

She shrugged one slender shoulder. "My father wanted all of us to know the business inside and out. I suppose he thought by starting us out young, we would learn what made Jarrod Ridge the premier resort in Aspen."

He could tell by the tensing of her muscles and the tight tone of her voice that they were skirting a touchy subject. "Do you think it would be all right for you to go riding tomorrow?" he asked, deciding to lighten the conversation. It was obvious she didn't care to talk about her father or the resort and he would have a much better chance of her agreeing to marry him if she were in a better mood. "I'd really like to show you the rest of the ranch. But if you think it would hurt you or the baby, we can wait," he hastened to add.

Her expression brightened. "I would really like that. I'm pretty sure it will be all right. I have a friend in California who rode her horses until she was six months pregnant and everything was fine."

"Great." He pressed a kiss to her forehead. "If you think what you saw of the ranch from the top of the ridge is beautiful, you'll really like seeing Rainbow Falls."

Her eyes twinkled with excitement, making him glad that he had thought of taking her to see it. "You have a waterfall on your property?"

"Yup."

"I love waterfalls. They're always so peaceful and relaxing. We even have the sound of a waterfall piped into the massage rooms at the spa."

"We'll have to get up early," he warned. "It will take us several hours to get there because of the terrain, but believe me, it's well worth it." For reasons he didn't understand and wasn't inclined to dwell on, he wanted to make the outing special for her. Thinking quickly, he added, "I thought we could pack a few sandwiches and have lunch by the falls."

"That sounds absolutely wonderful, Shane." She

covered her mouth with her hand to hide a yawn. "I can't wait."

"I think you'll have to." He chuckled. "Aside from the fact that it's already dark outside, you'd probably fall asleep in the saddle before we rode out of the ranch yard."

"You're probably right." She yawned again. "For the past few days, it seems that I can't get enough sleep."

"Is that because of the pregnancy, too?" He knew a whole lot more about pregnant mares than he did about pregnant women, but he figured it could be the reason behind her fatigue.

"I assume that's the reason," she said, resting her head against his chest.

Shane tightened his arms around her and lowering his head, covered her mouth with his for a quick kiss. Then, reluctantly stepping back, he turned toward the kitchen counter. "Why don't you go into the living room and put your feet up while I load the dishwasher and clean up?"

"Are you sure I can't help?" she asked, sounding tired.

"Positive. It won't take but a few minutes." He rinsed their plates and started stacking them in the dishwasher. "There is one thing you could do for me, though."

"What's that?"

"Turn on the sports channel and see if you can

catch who won the game this afternoon between the Rockies and the Cardinals."

"You're a baseball fan?"

Looking at her over his shoulder, he grinned. "I like baseball as much as the next guy. But this game is kind of special. I have a bet going with Cactus and I'd like to see who wins. He thinks the Cardinals will sweep the Rockies in this three-game series and I say they won't."

Laughing, she shook her head as she started toward the living room. "Men and their sports."

As he started the dishwasher, he couldn't help but think about how fast his plans had changed. When he had first come up with the idea of bringing Lissa to the ranch for the weekend, he had thought they would be spending the majority of their time within the confines of his bedroom. But that had changed in the blink of an eye with her announcement that she was going to have his baby.

Now, even though it made him as jumpy as a day-old colt, his main priority was convincing her to let him do the right thing by her and the baby. He wiped off the counter, then turning out the kitchen light, headed for the living room.

He had three days of uninterrupted time with her to figure out how to get her to say yes. Given her argument about their not knowing enough about each other, it probably wasn't going to be easy.

Smiling to himself as he walked down the hall, he decided he was more than ready for the challenge.

His personal code of honor demanded that he make her his wife and help her raise their child. And there wasn't a doubt in his mind that before he took her back to Aspen, she would agree to be just that.

Three

When Shane turned off the television, Melissa asked, "How much money did you win from your housekeeper?"

"None. If he had won, I was going to have to cook for the next month." Shane laughed. "But since he lost, the old boy is going to have to keep the driveway cleared of snow until spring."

"How old is Cactus?" she asked, hoping he was younger than Shane made him sound.

"I'm not sure," he said as he rose from the couch to take her hand in his. "He's a little sensitive about his age, but I'm pretty sure he's at least seventy and probably a few years older than that."

"He's that old and you're going to make him get

out in the cold to clear the snow?" she asked, allowing him to help her to her feet. She didn't like the idea of Shane taking advantage of the older gentleman. "Tell me you're going to take pity on him and let him out of this stupid bet."

"Not on your life." Grinning, he shook his head. "I don't feel the least bit sorry for him. He'll be on a tractor with a heated cab, a built-in CD player that he can crank up as loud as he wants with his favorite bluegrass music, and if I know Cactus, he'll have a Thermos of Irish coffee to keep him company."

"You make it sound like he was going to win either way."

Shane nodded as they climbed the stairs. "We go through this every fall. He'll come up with a bet he knows he can't win in order to do something he enjoys."

She didn't understand that kind of logic. "Then why doesn't he just volunteer for the job?"

"Because that's not how the old guy works," he explained. "When his arthritis started making it hard for him to do some of the ranch work, I knew he didn't want to leave the ranch. It's been his home for as long as I can remember. So I started complaining about needing someone to cook and take care of the house." Shane grinned. "I didn't really need anyone to do that, and he knew it. But he couldn't come right out and ask me for the job."

"So that's when the bets started?" she guessed.

Shane nodded. "He bet me that I couldn't beat his

time at saddling a horse. If he won, I had to buy him a new pair of boots and if I won, he would take the housekeeping job."

She liked that Shane would go to those lengths to preserve the older man's dignity. It told her a lot more about his character than he realized.

"You did it to save his pride."

"Exactly." Chuckling, Shane opened the door to the room he had shown her earlier. "So, with this latest bet, he not only gets to drive the tractor and pretend he's doing ranch work again, he has something to gripe about while he's doing it. And if there's anything he likes better than complaining, I don't know of it. He got his nickname because he's prickly as a cactus."

Melissa smiled as she entered the room. "He sounds like quite a colorful character."

"He is." Leaning one shoulder against the door-frame, Shane folded his arms across his wide chest. "He can be an ornery old cuss, but he's got a heart of solid gold. I'll make sure you get to meet him sometime."

"I'd like that." When he stood there as if he waited for something, she rose up on tiptoes to kiss his cheek. "Good night."

Before she could back away, he put his arms around her. "It will be once we go to my room."

"I don't understand." With his strong arms around her and the feel of his hard body pressed to hers, she suddenly felt winded. "If you wanted me to spend the night in your room…why did you put my case…in here?"

"I thought you might like to have the privacy this afternoon when you freshened up," he said, nuzzling the side of her neck. "I never intended for you to sleep here."

When his lips skimmed the hollow below her ear, a tingle raced up her spine. "Oh, I thought—"

"—I'd want you to leave my bed once we'd made love," he finished for her. "Not a chance, angel."

That wasn't what she had been thinking, but it was better than telling him that she thought he had lost interest in her now that she was pregnant. Some men couldn't get away from a woman fast enough when they learned of an unplanned pregnancy. Not knowing him any better than she did, what else was she to think?

But apparently she had been wrong about his desire waning. She sighed. It was just one more example of their lack of knowledge about each other, not to mention a serious breakdown in communication.

Before she could point that out, he asked, "Where's your bag? I'll take it to my room."

Taking a step back, she walked over to open one of the dresser drawers and removed her nightshirt. "After I unpacked, I put it in the closet."

He frowned as he pointed to the garment she held. "I've never known you to wear nightclothes."

"That's because you always left my place before I put them on," she shot back. "And since you seemed surprised to learn that I do wear a nightshirt, I assume you don't wear anything to bed."

"Nope," he said, grinning. "I don't like the encumbrance."

She shook her head. "This is what I was talking about earlier, Shane. If we had spent more time getting to know each other, we would know these things."

"You never wanted me to spend the night because you were afraid someone at the resort might find out and start gossiping about it," he pointed out.

She couldn't argue with him about that. It had been at her insistence that he leave Willow Lodge each night after they'd made love.

"But that's water under the bridge now," he said, shrugging.

Too tired to debate the issue any further, she nodded. "I suppose you're right."

He put his arm around her shoulders and steered her out into the hall. "I'll help you move your things to my room in the morning before we leave. Right now, we need to get to bed. We'll have to be up early if we're going to have lunch at the falls tomorrow."

When he led her into his bedroom and turned on the bedside lamp, she took a moment to look around. A lot could be learned from someone's personal space.

She wasn't at all surprised to see the large room was decorated in the same rustic, masculine style as the downstairs. A king-size log bed with a Native American–print comforter and pillows dominated the room. The bright colors of the matching drapes contrasted perfectly with the dark log walls and heavy, peeled-log dresser and chest of drawers.

If she had ever had any doubts about Shane being the quintessential cowboy, they were gone now. One look at his choice of decor was all it took to know that he was a lot like the land he loved—rugged and a little wild. The type of man that was dangerous to a woman's peace of mind. The very type women just couldn't seem to resist.

"How long has your family owned the ranch?" she asked.

"A little over a hundred and twenty-five years." He unbuttoned his shirt. "Hasn't your family owned Jarrod Ridge about as long?"

Fascinated by the play of his chest muscles when Shane shrugged out of the shirt, it took a moment for her to realize what he had asked. "Y-yes, my father's great great-grandfather started it and every generation since has expanded the business."

"What do you think your generation will add to the resort?" he asked, unbuckling his belt and reaching for the button at the waistband of his jeans.

"I don't know," she said absently. She was far too engrossed in watching him reveal his magnificent body to worry about what would happen at Jarrod Ridge.

When he pushed the denim down his thighs, her heart skipped a beat. She had watched him strip off his clothes many times since they began their affair.

She had even helped him take them off a few times, but the sight of his well-developed physique never failed to take her breath away.

"Aren't you going to change?" he asked as he reached for the waistband of his boxer briefs.

He either didn't know the effect he had on her or he was intentionally trying to drive her crazy. She suspected it was the latter.

Suddenly feeling as if she would burst into tears and not entirely certain why, Melissa quickly took off her clothes and pulled the nightshirt on. Walking around to the right side of the bed, she got in and closed her eyes. She was on Shane's ranch, in his bed and pregnant with his baby. It was all too much to comprehend.

Overwhelmed by the events of the day and completely exhausted, she couldn't stop a tear from slipping from beneath her lashes. She swiped it away with the back of her hand and turned onto her side in hopes that he hadn't noticed.

"Lissa, are you crying?"

"N-no."

She felt the other side of the bed dip as Shane stretched out beside her. A moment later, he wrapped her in his arms and turned her to face him.

"What's wrong, angel? Why are you crying?"

His concerned tone and the feel of him holding her so tenderly against him was all it took for the floodgates to open. Sobbing her heart out and unable to stop herself, she clung to him as the torrent of emotion ran its course.

"I—I don't know…why…that happened," she said when she was finally able to get her vocal cords to work. She had never been more embarrassed in her entire life.

"I think I do," he said as his hand continued to stroke her hair in a soothing manner. "You've had a hell of a day and you're so tired you can barely keep your eyes open."

His understanding words and the gentle tone of his deep voice helped ease some of her humiliation. "You're probably right. I think this has quite possibly been the most stressful day I have ever endured."

He reached over to switch off the lamp. Then, cradling her to him, he kissed her so tenderly another wave of tears threatened.

"Try to get some sleep, angel." His arms tightened around her. "It's all going to work out. I give you my word on that."

Too exhausted to think about everything that had happened since her return to Aspen two months ago for the reading of her father's will, Melissa snuggled against Shane and closed her eyes. Maybe with the morning light things would be clearer. Maybe then she would be able to cope with the fact that her life had spun completely out of control and there didn't seem to be a single thing she could do to stop it.

When Shane led the gelding out of the barn and over to the fence, he smiled. "Does this horse look familiar?"

Lissa's blue eyes twinkled with excitement. "He looks just like Smoky Joe."

"That's because he's old Smoky's little brother," he said, handing her the reins. After hearing that the blue roan had been her favorite at Jarrod Ridge, Shane purposely chose the horse for her to ride to Rainbow Falls.

"Thank you," she said as she softly stroked the horse's velvet muzzle. "What's his name?"

"He's registered with the American Quarter Horse Association as Smoke Storm, but we just call him Stormy." Walking back into the barn to get a saddle and blanket from the tack room, Shane returned to placed the saddle over the top fence rail. Then, smoothing the saddle blanket over the gelding's back, he added, "I don't want you to worry that he might be more than you can handle. In spite of his name, there's nothing stormy about him." He picked up the saddle and positioned it on the blanket. "I've seen kittens with more piss and vinegar than this guy."

Lissa smiled as she hugged the animal's neck. "Smoky Joe was that way, too. You could do just about anything with him."

Shane nodded. "That's why we bred the same mare and stallion several different times. The colts they foaled were all good-natured and perfect for people who aren't used to riding a lot."

"In other words, perfect for the inexperienced guests at Jarrod Ridge," she guessed.

He pulled the cinch tight. "That was the idea."

While Lissa and Stormy got to know each other, Shane quickly saddled his sorrel stallion. "Need a leg up?" he asked, turning to see if she needed help mounting the roan.

"I think I can get this," she said, slipping her booted foot into the stirrup.

He stepped behind her in case she had problems and immediately decided that he would have done well to take her at her word. When her perfect little blue-jeans-clad bottom bobbed in front of his face as she climbed onto the saddle, the air rushed out of his lungs like helium from an overinflated balloon.

Holding her soft body to his throughout the night, then waking up with her in his arms this morning without once making love to her, had been a true test of his control. But Lissa hadn't needed his lust. She had needed his comfort and he had been determined to give it to her or die trying.

Exhausted, emotionally spent and extremely vulnerable, she had tried to give the impression that she was fine. He knew differently and once he had taken her into his arms, she had finally let down her guard and accepted the support he had promised her. But not without considerable cost to his well-being.

With her breasts pressed to his chest and her delicate hand resting on his flank, he had spent the entire night aroused. And if that hadn't been enough to send him hovering on the brink of insanity, he had awakened this morning with one of her long, slender legs intimately lodged against his overly sensitive groin.

That had sent him straight into the bathroom for a cold shower. By the time he finally stepped from beneath the icy spray, his teeth had chattered uncontrollably and he would have bet everything he had that he could spit ice cubes on command.

Unfortunately, his gallantry was beginning to wear thin. He wasn't sure how much longer he would be able to play the consummate gentleman without going stark, raving mad.

"Earth to Shane. Come in please," Lissa said, bringing him back to the present.

"What?"

She laughed. "I asked if you are going to just stand there daydreaming or if we're going for a ride?"

"Uh, sorry," he muttered. He couldn't tell her that he had been thinking about how much he wanted to hold her, how much his body ached to be inside her. "There are a couple of different ways to get to the falls and I was trying to decide which would be the fastest," he said, thinking quickly. There was only one trail leading to the waterfall, but she didn't know that and he wasn't about to admit that he'd been fantasizing about stripping them both and making love to her until they both collapsed from exhaustion.

"How far is it to Rainbow Falls?" she asked as he mounted the stallion and they rode through the corral gate.

"It's only about three miles as the eagle flies, but having to skirt some of the steeper terrain and due to all of the bends in the river, it takes a few hours," he explained.

She gave him a wistful look. "I wish I had known about this trip before we left the lodge. I'd have brought my camera. I'm sure the scenery is going to be gorgeous."

He decided not to remind her that once he made her his wife, she would be able to take as many pictures of his ranch as she wanted, any time she wanted. But he wasn't a fool. If he did remind her of that fact, she would most likely come up with more ways they didn't know each other and be on the defensive.

That was the last thing he wanted. His plan hinged on the element of surprise. When he played his ace in the hole, he had no doubt he would have her agreeing to marry him faster than he could slap his own ass with both hands.

"Shane, this is absolutely breathtaking," Melissa said as they rode single file over the ridge and around a switchback into the upland valley.

"It isn't much good for pasturing the horses, but I like to camp out here occasionally," he said, leading the way down the slope.

"I love camping out," she said, remembering the wonderful time she'd had when her father allowed her to go on a couple of overnight trail rides with some of the resort's guests.

It had taken considerable thought on her part and several arguments with her father to convince him that she would be there to address any special needs of the Jarrod Ridge guests. He had finally relented, but only after she had pointed out that she would technically still be working for the resort and not just frittering away her time. God forbid that she did something with her time that she actually enjoyed, she thought, unable to keep from feeling resentful.

"What's wrong?" Shane called over his shoulder.

Jarred back to the present, she focused on the man riding the big red stallion ahead of her. "Nothing. Why do you ask?"

Stopping his horse, he turned in the saddle. "I've seen happier faces on condemned felons."

"The sun was in my eyes," she said, hoping he would drop the matter.

"If you say so." His expression told her that he wasn't buying her excuse, but to her relief, he let it go.

She didn't want to discuss the unreasonable demands Donald Jarrod had placed on his children. It was something she had spent her entire adult life trying to forget and she certainly didn't want to ruin an otherwise glorious day thinking about her childhood. Besides, she didn't know Shane well enough to share the dirt on a family that, up until her father's death and the subsequent discovery that she had an illegitimate half sister, had an impeccable reputation.

They rode in companionable silence for some time before he pointed to the river. "As soon as we go around this bend, you'll see Rainbow Falls just off to the right."

Riding side by side once they cleared the tree line, Melissa's attention once again turned to Shane. He was an expert horseman and handled the stallion with ease. But aside from admiring the way he sat the horse, she simply loved watching him.

With his black Resistol pulled down low on his brow to shade his eyes and a day-old growth of beard, he looked a little wild, possibly dangerous and totally delicious.

A tremor coursed through her and she had to remind herself that lusting after the man was not conducive to getting her life back under control. Not only had she become pregnant because of it, the physical attraction she had for him was in danger of transforming into something deeper, something more meaningful.

Even though what she felt for him was probably nothing more than a temporary infatuation, in the end it could still do a lot of emotional damage and leave behind some deep long-lasting scars.

As devastatingly handsome and charming as Shane was, he just wasn't the type of man for her. He had the reputation of moving from one woman to another, leaving a string of broken hearts in his wake. Given the circumstances they found themselves in now, that was one complication she could definitely do without.

He had made it clear right up front that he wasn't looking for a lasting commitment. Neither was she. She had her own business in California and she might be returning to her life there once the year required to obtain her inheritance was over. She'd reasoned that it was better not to look for anything deeper than a casual relationship until she had decided what she was going to do. After witnessing what some of her friends went through as they tried to maintain long-distance commitments, she had quickly decided it wasn't for her. Things never seemed to work out, and the hurt and disillusionment that went along with a breakup was something she definitely wanted to avoid.

Besides, she hadn't really taken Shane's proposal seriously. That's why she had dismissed outright his outrageous suggestion that they get married. It had to have been a knee-jerk reaction to the startling news, and once he had more time to think about it, she was certain he would see reason. He would probably even be relieved that she'd had the foresight to turn him down.

The sound of rushing water brought her out of her disturbing introspection and, looking up, Melissa realized they had ridden around the bend in the river and arrived at Rainbow Falls. It was everything Shane had told her and more.

Cascading from the ridge high above, the water fell a good seventy-five feet onto the massive boulders below, then slowing, it formed the lazy river that meandered across the valley floor. What caught and held her attention more than anything was the faint rainbow caused by the sun reflecting off the mist created by the falling water.

"It's absolutely beautiful," she said, understanding why it had been named Rainbow River.

"I was pretty sure you would like it." She could hear the satisfaction and pride in Shane's voice and knew he was pleased that she hadn't been disappointed.

They stopped the horses along the riverbank just out of the icy mist and dismounted. As soon as her feet hit the ground, her legs felt as if the tendons had been replaced with stretched-out rubber bands and her muscles had turned to Jell-O.

When she took a wobbly step, Shane was immediately at her side to support her. "Are you all right?"

Nodding, she took another tentative step. "I should go riding more often. Maybe then I would be in better condition."

Shane took her into his arms. "I think you're in great shape, angel." He laughed. "You'd have to be to twist yourself up like a Christmas bow in those yoga classes."

"Yoga is more about stretching and relaxing the muscles." Smiling, she enjoyed the feel of him holding her to him. "Horseback riding takes a certain amount of tensing the thigh muscles to help you stay balanced in the saddle."

"Your thigh muscles don't seem to be all that weak when you hold on to me," he said, nuzzling the side of her neck. His deep baritone sent shivers of excitement streaking up her spine and her legs threatened to fail her for an entirely different reason this time.

Before Melissa had the chance to respond to his suggestive words, his mouth came down on hers and she forgot all about her weak knees or the internal lecture she had given herself about lusting after the man. All she wanted, could even think about, was the feel of his lips moving over hers with such gentle care.

When he used his tongue to coax her to allow him entry to her tender inner recesses, she wrapped her arms around his waist and held on for dear life. As he teased and coaxed her to answer his exploration with one of her own, a lazy heat spread throughout her body and her lower stomach tightened with the ache of unfulfilled desire.

But the spell that seemed to hold her in its grip was broken when he moved his hands to lift the tail of her pink T-shirt and the icy mist coated her bare abdomen. The breeze had shifted, carrying the spray farther than when they first got off the horses and they were both getting wet.

Shane quickly moved them out of the way, but the mood was effectively shattered and not a moment too soon. What on earth had she been thinking?

She had forgotten all about why going blithely along as if nothing had happened wasn't going to solve her dilemma. They hadn't fully discussed or made any decisions about her being pregnant, and that was something they were going to have to address in the very near future. The pregnancy couldn't be hidden indefinitely. Once she started showing, people were going to start talking and asking questions. She wanted to be ready with some answers when they did.

Unfortunately, it was always this way when Shane held her, kissed her. Sound judgment and common sense seemed to take a backseat to the passion and desire he created within her.

"I think we'd better…break out those sandwiches we made…before we left your house," she said, trying to catch her breath. "I'm starting to…get hungry."

His mouth curved upward in a wicked grin. "To tell you the truth, Lissa, I am starved to death right now. But my hunger hasn't got a damned thing to do with food."

Doing her best to ignore the excitement that his candid comment evoked, she walked over to the roan and began unpacking one of the saddlebags. "You, Mr. McDermott, are incorrigible."

He laughed as he helped her spread a blanket for their picnic. "More like insatiable, angel."

"That may be, but do the best you can to contain yourself," she said, smiling as she carried their lunch to the blanket.

Kneeling at the edge of the fleece, she avoided his intense blue gaze as she placed the sandwiches on plates, then opened two small bottles of apple juice. If she looked at him, there was a very good chance she would abandon her resolve and that was something she couldn't afford to let happen.

"We have things to talk about and decisions to make," she said, taking a sip from her juice.

His expression turning serious, Shane lowered himself to sit on the blanket beside her. "Let's put a hold on that for right now. We'll have plenty of time to make our plans tomorrow." Smiling, he reached for a sandwich. "You need to take today to relax and regroup, anyway. Yesterday was a pretty rough day for you."

It was the first reference he had made to her meltdown the night before, and she was grateful that he didn't seem overly interested in pursuing it now. "Maybe you're right."

"I know I am," he said, sounding so darned sure of himself, she wasn't sure whether she should kiss him or take something and bop him with it.

Either way, she decided to take his advice. There would be plenty of time tomorrow to figure what to do about a carefree affair that had unexpectedly become a very serious issue.

Four

The first shadows of evening had just begun to stretch across the valley when Shane and Lissa rode back into the ranch yard. All in all, it had been a pretty good day, he decided as they dismounted. He had been more than a little pleased by her reaction to his ranch and looked forward to showing her more when they had time.

"I've been thinking that supper in front of the television would be nice tonight," he said, leading their horses into the stable. "We can watch a movie on one of the satellite channels or pop a DVD in the player." Unsaddling the stallion, he carried the tack and blanket into the tack room, then returned to the center aisle of the stable to do the same with the roan. "Although, I think I had better warn you. I don't have much in the way of romantic movies in my collection."

"Why doesn't that surprise me?" she asked, laughing as she reached for a brush to groom the gelding. "I have to admit though, a night of vegging out does sound nice. And whatever you choose to watch is fine with me. I'll probably fall asleep before the opening credits even get started."

Finished with brushing the stallion, Shane led the animal down to his stall, then returned for Stormy. "Why don't you go on to the house and take a hot shower? It will only take me another few minutes to feed and water the horses."

Without waiting to see if she took him up on his suggestion, Shane walked Stormy to his stall, then set about giving the animals oats and filling their water troughs. He was surprised when he turned around to find that Lissa had sat down on a bale of straw beside the tack room door to wait for him.

"I thought you were going to take a shower and change," he said, walking up beside her.

Shrugging, she smiled. "I thought we could go back to the house together."

He liked the sound of that and without hesitation, he picked her up and sat down to settle her on his lap. Her arms automatically circled his neck and she laid her head on his shoulder.

Damn, but he loved holding her like this. "Legs still a bit wobbly from riding so much?"

"A little. But not as bad as the first time I dismounted." She snuggled closer. "Thank you for today," she said softly. "I really enjoyed seeing your ranch and Rainbow Falls. It's all very beautiful."

Her warm breath whispering over his neck and the feel of her cradled against him sent his hormones racing. His arousal was not only immediate, it left him feeling light-headed from its intensity.

"I'm glad you had a good time," he said, shifting to a more comfortable position.

"I've been thinking, Shane."

He didn't like the sound of her tentative tone. "About what?"

"This weekend should probably be our last time seeing each other."

Her voice was so quiet he wasn't sure he had heard her correctly. But a bucket of ice water couldn't have been more effective at putting an end to his overly active libido.

Sitting her up on his lap, he met her gaze head-on. "You want to explain yourself? What do you mean this is our last time together?"

She sighed. "Jarrod Ridge is a family-oriented resort. Some of the older investors would likely take a dim view of our having an affair."

"What do you think is going to happen when they find out you're pregnant out of wedlock?" he shot back. The way he saw it, they'd take the news a whole lot better and be less likely to condemn if she had the baby's daddy standing beside her.

She nibbled on her lower lip a moment before shaking her head. "I've thought about that, too. I'm hoping they won't find out."

A chill raced up his spine. She wasn't talking about…

"I'll have to check with our attorney, Christian Hanford, to see if there's a way to keep from losing my inheritance if I move back to California. But having the baby out there would keep the talk down around the resort," she said, oblivious to the fact that she had damned near given him a coronary before she finished explaining. "You and my family will be the only ones who know that I've had a child. I know they'll keep that kind of news quiet in order to keep from jeopardizing our business."

Why did everyone's opinion matter so much to her? For that matter, why did the whole family protect the Jarrod Ridge reputation as if it were as valuable as the gold in Fort Knox?

"Why the hell are you protecting the resort above all else, Lissa?" he asked before he could stop himself. But once the words were out, he couldn't really say he regretted the question.

She looked stunned. "What do you mean?"

"Why are you scared to death about what everyone is going to say or think?"

Shane knew he was treading on dangerous ground, but he had a feeling that it had been drilled into her as a child that appearances were everything and the reputation of the resort came before anything else.

Even if it meant sacrificing her own happiness or well-being.

Her body stiffened and he knew he had hit the nail on the head. "My father's death caused enough upheaval. Jarrod Ridge doesn't need unrest among the people with a vested interest in its success," she insisted. "We need their funding to bring more events to the resort."

He could tell she was avoiding having to answer his questions. He decided to let that slide for now. But eventually she was going to have to stop putting that damned resort and its precious reputation ahead of her own wants and needs. And if it took him having to bring that to her attention, he was up for the challenge.

"I'm one of the investors in the resort and I couldn't care less what the majority of those old goats think."

He pulled her close and wondered what kind of childhood she'd had. If being put to work at the age of eight and her unrealistic concerns about gossip were any indication, it had to have been miserable.

"But we aren't going to talk about any of that now," he said, determined to change the subject. "This afternoon, we made an agreement to get this all straightened out tomorrow. I'm going to hold you to that."

Deciding not to give her the opportunity to argue the point further, he captured her mouth with his. Resistant at first, he felt her begin to relax against him as he traced her perfect coral lips with his tongue, then coaxed her to open for him. His blood heated and his body reacted as it always did when she was in his arms. When he stroked her tongue with his, he could tell from her soft moan that she was as turned on as he was.

Unfortunately, sitting on a bale of straw in a stable had to be one of the least sensual places on earth. Cursing himself as nine kinds of a fool for starting something he couldn't finish until they went to the house, he groaned and reluctantly broke the kiss.

"I think it's about time we took that hot shower," he said, setting her on her feet.

"We?" she asked as he rose to take her hand in his and hurry her toward the stable doors.

He didn't even try to stop his wicked grin. "I've decided it's about time for the ranch to 'go green.' We'll save water by showering together."

When they reached the house, Shane stopped only long enough to remove their boots, then led Melissa toward the stairs. No matter how foolish it might be, she willingly followed him straight into the master bathroom.

She was determined not to think about this weekend being the end of their affair or the loneliness she would suffer once it was over. It might not be smart, but she wanted to store up the memory of his tender touch and the strength of his lovemaking. She would need them on those lonely nights that lay ahead of her once they stopped seeing each other.

"You do realize you're way overdressed for a shower, don't you?" he asked, his blue eyes twinkling with mischief as he closed the door.

She smiled. "I could say the same thing about you, Cowboy."

"Really?" He reached for the snaps on his chambray shirt as he took a step toward her. "I'm pretty sure I can remedy that."

"Don't." She reached up to remove his hat, then hanging it on the doorknob, took his hands in hers and lowered them to his sides. "Let me see if I can take care of it for you."

Releasing the first closure, she kissed his tanned collarbone. "That wasn't too difficult," she said, lightly skimming her nails along his skin as her fingers traveled on to the next snap. She flicked it open, then pressed a kiss to the newly exposed skin. "Neither was that."

His abdominal muscles contracted when she continued on to the next one. She smiled as she slowly released each closure to nibble and kiss his perfect torso. "I think I'm starting to get the hang of this."

"Oh, I would say you've become quite proficient at it." His voice was husky and when she glanced up, the heated look in his blue gaze stole her breath.

As they continued to stare at each other, she finished unsnapping his shirt and tugged the tail of it from the waistband of his jeans. Parting the lapels,

Melissa moved to push the garment over his shoulders and down his arms.

Her heart skipped a beat as she gazed at his sculpted chest and abdomen. Unable to resist, she touched the hard ridges of his stomach with her fingertip, then traced the thin line of hair from his navel to where it disappeared into the waistband of his jeans. She was rewarded with his sharp intake of breath.

"You've got a good start there, angel," he encouraged. "Don't stop now."

"I don't intend to." Unbuckling his leather belt, she shook her head. "I was always taught not to quit until a job was finished." She released the button at the top of his jeans and toyed with the metal tab below. "And to make sure the job was done to the best of my ability."

Slowly, intentionally, she pulled the zipper downward. By the time she eased it over his persistent arousal to the bottom of his fly, Melissa wasn't certain which one of them was having more trouble drawing their next breath.

"Oh my, Mr. McDermott," she teased as she lightly touched the bulging cotton of his boxer briefs. "You seem to have a bit of a problem."

His big body jerked as if an electrical charge had coursed through it. "You caused my current dilemma. Now what are you going to do about it?" he asked through gritted teeth.

The feral light in his eyes caused a delicious

warmth to spread throughout her being. "What would you suggest I do?"

"Finish what you started."

Smiling, she put her hands on his sides, then slipping her fingers inside both waistbands slid his jeans and underwear over his hips and down his legs. He quickly stepped out of them, then kicked them to the side.

She took a moment to appreciate his perfection. Her heart skipped several beats as she let her gaze slide from his handsome face down his torso and beyond. Muscles developed by years of hard ranch work padded his shoulders and chest and his stomach was taut with ridges of toned sinew. Every cell in her body tingled as she took in the beauty of Shane's male body and his strong, proud arousal.

"I love your body," she found herself murmuring.

"It was made just for yours, angel." Lifting the hem of her T-shirt, his grin was filled with such promise it sent goose bumps shimmering over her skin. "Since you've been so nice and helped me out, I think it's only fair that I return the favor."

"I think so, too," she said.

As methodically as she had removed his clothing, Shane removed hers and tossed them into the growing pile on the bathroom floor. When he removed the last scrap of silk and lace, he stood back.

"You're absolutely gorgeous, Lissa." He pulled her into his arms, and the feel of hard masculine flesh touching her much softer feminine skin caused a need within her so deep it reached all the way to her soul.

"I think we'd better take that shower while we still have the strength," he said, his voice hoarse.

She waited until he adjusted the water, then stepped under the luxurious, multiheaded spray. When he joined her, Shane turned her away from him, then reached for a bottle of shampoo. As his large hands began to gently massage her scalp and work the shampoo down the long strands, Melissa didn't think she had ever felt anything more sensual than having him wash her hair.

Neither spoke as he rinsed away the last traces of shampoo, then reached for the soap. Working the herbal-scented bar into a rich lather, he held her gaze as he slowly smoothed his hands over every inch of her body and by the time he was finished she felt more cherished than she ever had in her entire life.

"My turn," she said, taking the soap from him.

Treating him to the same sensuous exploration, she took the time to commit to memory every muscle and cord of his perfect physique. When she finally touched him intimately, she watched him tightly close his eyes. His head fell back and a groan rumbled up from deep in his chest a moment before he took the soap from her, rinsed them both thoroughly, then gathered her to him.

He lowered his head and the moment his mouth came down to cover hers, she put her arms around his wide shoulders and her eyes drifted shut. She could feel herself being lifted and automatically brought her legs up to wrap them around his lean hips. They fit against each other perfectly, and when he entered her with one smooth stroke, Melissa reveled in the feeling of being one with him.

As water sprayed over them from all sides, their wet bodies moved together in perfect unison, and all too soon, she felt herself start to climb toward the peak of completion. Her muscles tensed as the need grew and intensified. Then, as if something inside of her broke free, pleasure filled every fiber of her being and stars danced behind her tightly closed eyes.

Almost immediately Shane's body surged within her a final time and he crushed her to him. She held him just as tightly as he rode out the storm and found his own shuddering release.

When she finally gained the strength to move, Melissa leaned back to look at his handsome face as he still held her to him. For the past couple of months, she had told herself their affair was strictly physical and she could walk away from it at any time with no regrets. She now realized that she had been deluding herself. From the moment he introduced himself at a meeting between her family and the Jarrod Ridge investors, she had not only been attracted to him physically, she had been drawn to his charming personality and easy sense of humor.

"You're amazing," he said, giving her a tender kiss as he lowered her to her feet. He turned off the shower, then helping her out of the enclosure, patted them both dry with a large, plush towel. "Why don't I pop a pizza in the oven and find something for us to watch on one of the movie channels, while you dry your hair and get dressed?" he asked as he wrapped the towel around her, then tucked it under her arms.

"That sounds wonderful," she said, realizing she was actually quite hungry.

He gave her a smile warm enough to melt the polar ice caps. "I'll meet you downstairs on the couch in about twenty minutes."

Feeling more relaxed than she had since taking the pregnancy test, Melissa picked up the hair dryer and turned it on. She wasn't going to think about their predicament, what they were going to do about it or that in less than two days she would no longer be enjoying a few stolen hours with Shane. Tonight she was going to concentrate on the moment and face tomorrow when it came.

"What's your life like out in California?" Shane asked as the movie he had selected for them ended.

The film's storyline had been about a woman returning to her hometown and the life she had left behind to do that. That got him to thinking. He knew what it had been like for Lissa since returning to Aspen for the reading of her father's will. She had to stay for at least one year and manage the Tranquility Spa in order to inherit her share of Jarrod Ridge. But her life in Los Angeles remained a complete mystery to him.

"Life in southern California is, in a word, hectic." She shrugged one slender shoulder. "I've been there since I started college and you would think I'd be used to the pace after all this time."

Her answer surprised him. "But you're not?"

"Not really." She shook her head and shifted on the couch to face him. "Everyone is always in such a hurry to get somewhere or to do something. Then, when they do accomplish whatever they set out to do, they are in a huge hurry to do something else."

"Life in the fast lane can be draining," he said, wondering why she had chosen to go to college so far from home. "But I think it's that way in most urban areas."

She nodded as she removed the fluffy tie holding her hair in a ponytail. "It's a little better in Malibu where I live now, but life still moves a lot faster than Aspen."

"That is a nice area." He had been to Malibu a few times and although it was way too crowded for his taste, Shane had found the view of the ocean to be beautiful. "Do you live near the beach?"

"I have a condo not too far from the Malibu Pier." She smiled. "I like living on the beach and my spa and yoga center, Serendipity, is only a couple of miles away. That's another plus for me."

"Who's running things while you're away?" he asked, reaching out to tuck a wayward strand of hair behind her ear. "I'm sure you left someone you could trust in charge."

He ran his index finger over her hair. He loved the feel of the silky golden threads against his skin. He drew in some much-needed air and forced himself to concentrate on what she was saying. Lissa felt it was important that they talk and learn about each other. Besides, if he was going to get her to go along with his plans of getting married, he was going to have to pay a little closer attention.

"I have two wonderful assistant managers." She smiled fondly. "Michael is very efficient at managerial duties and in the treatment room his hands are pure magic."

"Oh, really?" For reasons he didn't quite understand and wasn't ready to analyze, the only hands Shane wanted her to consider magical were his.

Her enthusiastic nod caused a slow burn to start in the pit of his stomach. "Michael warms the oil with his hands, then when he puts them on your body and starts kneading the muscles…" She closed her eyes and smiled as if imagining the man's hands on her. "…it's pure heaven."

The irritation in Shane's gut exploded into all-out anger and he couldn't figure out why. Maybe it had something to do with the fact that Lissa seemed to enjoy having the man's hands on her a little too much. It might even be the probability that she had been alone with the guy in a dimly lit room with nothing but a thin sheet draped over her nude body. Or more likely, it was a combination of all of it. Whatever the reason, he didn't like it one damned bit.

But Shane couldn't understand the proprietary feeling he had toward her. It wasn't as if he hadn't been with his share of women before Lissa returned to Aspen. It would be ridiculous of him to expect her to have gone without companionship before they started seeing each other. Yet he couldn't quite shake the territorial feeling that ran through him.

"Aren't some of the women who work for you just as good at giving massages?" he asked, wondering why she hadn't asked one of her female employees.

She nodded. "In their own way, yes, they are very good. But being a man, Michael naturally has more strength in his hands and gives a more thorough deep-tissue massage."

"How long has he worked for you?"

"Let's see, he and his life partner, Hector, moved from Florida into the condo below mine about three years ago, and I hired them both shortly after that," she said, looking pleased with herself. "I was really lucky to get them before another spa snapped them up. Besides Michael being the best masseuse I've ever seen, Hector is a master yoga instructor and conducts most of the yoga and meditation classes at Serendipity. He's my assistant manager for the yoga center."

Shane's anger cooled immediately when he realized neither of the men were interested in Lissa. The fact that he felt such relief was almost as disturbing to him as his possessiveness had been. He had never been the jealous type and couldn't imagine what the hell had gotten into him.

Deciding it was time for a change of topic, he asked, "Do you miss not living near the beach?"

"Absolutely," she said, nodding. "Listening to the waves is nice, especially at night when I'm ready to go to sleep. I like to sit on the beach sometimes and watch them roll in to shore. It reminds me of how small and insignificant my problems are compared to the big picture."

"Don't you miss watching the seasons change, angel?"

"They do change," she admitted. "But it's subtle and not nearly as big of a change as here. It's beautiful here in the fall." She grinned. "And I do love Aspen in the winter. There's nothing like flying down the mountain on a pair of skis after a new snow."

"You like the fresh powder?"

"Absolutely." She tilted her head. "What about you? Do you like to ski?"

He gave her a mischievous grin. "I have been known to tear it up on a few of the slopes around here. I've also done a little cross-country skiing."

Yawning, she leaned her head back against the couch. "I've missed being able to participate in the winter activities we have in the mountains."

"They have some nice skiing in California," he reminded her.

"Yes, but I would have to drive several hours to

get there." She smiled. "I like having a ski slope practically in my backyard."

"Then why did you go to college in California in the first place?" he asked before he could stop himself.

Shane had a feeling it had something to do with her getting away from home and the control of Donald Jarrod. But she'd shied away from discussing her relationship with her father, and from her expression, she wasn't interested in discussing it now.

She hesitated as if choosing a suitable answer. "I was young and wanted to spread my wings a bit." Hiding another yawn behind her hand, she gave him a sheepish grin. "I think I need to go up to bed before I fall asleep right here."

He knew she was making an excuse to escape before he had the opportunity to ask any more questions. "You're probably right." Turning off the television, he rose to his feet, then helped her to hers. "What do you say we go upstairs and see just how good I am at giving a massage?"

"But I don't have a problem with tightness in my shoulders or neck," she said as he led her toward the stairs.

"Angel, I wasn't talking about massaging your back." He couldn't stop his wicked grin. "The areas I had in mind are on the front side of your body and a whole lot more interesting."

Shane lay staring at the ceiling long after the woman in his arms drifted off to sleep. The evening had been perfect and given him a glimpse of what life could be like once he and Lissa were married.

Married. The word alone should have had him running for the hills, and he still couldn't quite believe that he was actually going to take the plunge.

Two days ago, the idea of marriage and having a child never crossed his mind. It was simply something he had never allowed himself to contemplate. He had witnessed the hell his father went through when his mother left and that was more than enough to convince Shane he wanted no part of the institution.

He could remember the nights he had lain in bed as a small boy listening to his mother and father argue about how unhappy she was living out in the middle of nowhere. Eventually her pleading for his father to sell the ranch and move them all to a metropolitan area had turned to threats of her leaving.

Then, one day when he was nine, Shane came home from school to find his mother gone and his father passed out with an empty whiskey bottle at his feet. Cactus had stepped in to watch over him and when his father finally sobered up after a two-month bender, Shane asked several times where his mother was. "Gone" was all he could get out of his father each time he asked. Shane finally gave up and stopped asking.

But Hank McDermott was never the same after that. Other than being there to raise his son and instill a strong set of values in him, it was as if his dad had quit caring about everything else and reminded

Shane of a horse that had its spirit broken. Once full of life, his father rarely left the ranch and removed everything in the house that hinted a woman had ever inhabited the place.

Shane had never wanted to give that kind of power over him to any woman. Never wanted a child of his to lie awake at night wondering where his mother was and why he never heard from her again. But with Lissa's announcement that she was pregnant, he suddenly found himself determined to do the very thing he had vowed never to do—get married.

Glancing at her head resting on his shoulder, he took a deep breath and tried to relax. As long as he kept everything in perspective and his feelings for her under control, everything should be fine.

He would be a good provider, a faithful husband to her and a loving father to their child. That's all any woman could ask of a man and all Shane was ready or willing to give.

Five

"It's about time you hauled your sorry butt out of bed."

At the sound of the elderly gentleman's comment, Melissa stopped abruptly just inside the kitchen doorway. Standing at the stove, wearing nothing but a pair of long underwear and boots that had seen better days, the man had his back to her and apparently only heard her approach. She assumed he was Shane's housekeeper, Cactus, and he obviously thought that Shane had come downstairs for breakfast.

How could she let him know that she wasn't who he thought she was without startling him?

When he suddenly turned around, they both jumped. "God's nightgown! Where in the name of Sam Hill did you come from?"

"You must be Cactus," she said, unsure of what else to say. "Shane's told me a lot about you."

"Well, he never told me a damn…danged thing about you," he stammered. "If he had, I sure wouldn't be standin' here in nothin' but my long johns." His wrinkled cheeks turned fiery red above his grizzled beard. "Excuse me, ma'am. I'll go get myself decent."

The man disappeared into a room off the kitchen as quickly as his arthritic legs would allow. A moment later, Shane walked up behind her to wrap his arms around her waist.

"How did you manage to get breakfast started so fast?" he asked, kissing her nape.

Her skin tingled from the contact. "I didn't. It appears that your housekeeper, Cactus, has arrived home a little earlier than expected."

He sighed as he rested his chin on her shoulder. "I'm sorry, Lissa. I should have known this would happen. Whenever he goes to see his sister they always get into an argument and he ends up coming home early about half the time."

"It doesn't matter." She turned within the circle of his arms to smile up at him. "Cactus probably doesn't know anyone affiliated with the resort. Besides, I seriously doubt that he would tell them I was here, even if he did."

Shane kissed the tip of her nose. "Why is that, angel?"

"Because he knows I could tell them I caught him

cooking breakfast in his long underwear," she said, laughing. "If his blush was any indication, I think I embarrassed him all the way to the roots of his snow-white hair."

Rolling his eyes, Shane shook his head. "He definitely marches to the beat of his own drum. But don't worry. He'll get over it."

"Boy, I got a bone to pick with you," Cactus groused as he limped back into the room. "Why didn't you tell me you were gonna have a lady friend comin' for a visit this weekend?"

"I didn't figure it would matter, since you weren't supposed to be here," Shane answered, unaffected by the older man's irritation. Releasing her, he walked over to the coffeemaker. "Have a seat at the table, Lissa, while I pour us a cup of coffee. Lissa, this is Cactus Parsons, my housekeeper and the orneriest old cuss you'd ever care to meet."

"It's nice to meet you, Cactus," she said, smiling.

He nodded. "Ma'am."

Remembering something one of her friends had mentioned about not drinking caffeinated beverages while pregnant, Lissa shook her head. "Thank you, but I think I'll pass on the coffee."

When Shane walked over to sit beside her at the table, Cactus asked, "How do you like your eggs, gal?"

"Say scrambled," Shane whispered. "That's the only way he knows how to cook them."

"I heard that, and it ain't true," the old gentleman retorted. "I know how to put cheese in 'em or if your lady friend would like onions and green peppers, I can make 'em that way, too."

Shane laughed. "But they're still scrambled."

"It don't matter," Cactus insisted, his toothless grin wide. "They're still different than just plain old eggs."

Having grown up in the house where teasing and good-natured banter hadn't existed, Lissa enjoyed listening to the exchange between the two men. It told her a lot about the kind of man Shane was.

Besides going out of his way to preserve an old man's dignity by making bets they both knew were a complete farce, Shane went along with and even encouraged the man's complaints because he knew it made Cactus happy.

That was something her father certainly would have never done for one of his employees. For that matter, he hadn't bothered to do anything even remotely similar to that for his own children.

There wasn't a single time in her life that she could remember her father teasing or playing with her or her brothers. He had reminded them on a daily basis from the time they were old enough to listen that if they weren't excelling academically or working to somehow improve Jarrod Ridge, they were letting themselves down and disappointing him.

"Here you go, gal," Cactus said, interrupting her

thoughts as he placed a plate of bacon and eggs in front of her.

As soon as the plate touched the table, the food that had smelled so delicious only a few moments before caused a terrible queasiness in the pit of her stomach. Glancing at Shane, she watched his easy expression turn to one of concern and she knew she must look as ill as she felt.

Unable to make an excuse for leaving the table, Melissa jumped from the chair and ran as fast as she could for the stairs. She barely managed to make it into the master bathroom and slam the door before falling to her knees.

She had never in all of her twenty-six years been as sick as she was at that moment. If the fact that she was pregnant hadn't sunk in before, it certainly had became very real now.

Feeling as if the blood in his veins had turned to ice water, Shane took the stairs two at a time as he chased Lissa. What the hell was wrong with her?

She had seemed fine when they got up and came downstairs for breakfast. Then, without warning, she'd turned ghostly pale and bolted from the room like a racehorse coming out of the starting gate.

As soon as he entered his bedroom he heard her and found the bathroom door locked. "Lissa, let me in," he demanded.

"Go…away…Shane." Her voice sounded weak and shaky.

"Not until I know you're going to be all right." If he had to, he would break the damned door down. But he wasn't going anywhere until he found out what was wrong with her.

"I think…I have…morning sickness," she said, sounding downright miserable. "Please leave…me… alone so I…can die…in peace."

Feeling completely useless, Shane drew in a deep breath and walked over to sit on the end of the bed while he waited for her nausea to run its course. He felt guilty. If not for one of his swimmers, she wouldn't be in there feeling as if death would be a blessing.

He rested his forearms on his knees and stared down at his loosely clasped hands. He wished there was something he could do for her, but he was at a total loss. Horses didn't suffer through morning sickness and, since he never intended to have a wife and kids, he had never bothered to learn more than the basics about human pregnancies. Now he was going to have to play catch-up and learn all he could on the subject.

Several minutes later as he sat there mentally compiling a list of things that he wanted to research, he heard the bathroom lock click open and Lissa slowly opened the door. His heart slammed against his ribs at her appearance.

She looked as though she had just been through hell. Her usual peaches-and-cream complexion was still a pasty white, perspiration dotted her forehead and her long blond hair hung limp around her shoulders.

"I asked for privacy," she said, sounding completely spent.

"I gave you as much as I thought you needed." He might fall short with his lack of knowledge, but there was no way he would have left her on her own and gone back downstairs. "Does morning sickness last the entire length of the pregnancy or is it a short-term thing?"

Walking over to sit down on the bed beside him, she shook her head. "Every pregnancy is different. Some women have it for the entire nine months and others aren't bothered by it at all. My friend in California only had a problem with morning sickness for a month or so before it disappeared."

Nine months of being sick every morning? Just the thought made his skin crawl. In his estimation even a day or two was way too much.

"Is there something the doctor can give you to keep it from happening?" he asked, hoping there was.

He put his arm around her shoulders and tucked her to his side. Surely in this day and age there had to be something to help a woman get through it.

"I think there is medication to help with the nausea, but since I haven't been to the doctor yet, it's irrelevant at the moment." She yawned. "Maybe it would be a good idea for you to take me back to the resort this afternoon."

Shane didn't have to think twice about his answer. "No way." Rising to his feet, he pulled her up with him, then walked her around to the side of the bed. "There's no one there to take care of you and as sick as you are, I don't want you being by yourself."

"If I need something or someone, I can call Erica," she said, referring to the half sister the Jarrod children had learned of during the reading of their father's will.

"We both know you wouldn't do that," he stated, pulling back the comforter. "Your sister would want an explanation, and you aren't ready to give her one." He motioned for her to lie down. "I told you that I was going to see you through all of this and that is exactly what I intend to do, angel. Now, stretch out and take a nap. Maybe you'll feel better when you wake up."

"You're not going to be a bully about this, are you?" she asked. He thought she might dig her heels in and try to resist him telling her what to do, but to his satisfaction she climbed into bed. "Because if you are, I'm not—"

"Only if I have to be, to make sure I keep you and the baby safe and well," he said, careful to keep his voice gentle. Pulling the cover up over her, he sat down on the side of the bed. "Now get some rest, Lissa." It was only after he kissed her smooth cheek that he realized she had already fallen asleep.

Shane wasn't certain when he had developed the fierce protectiveness that coursed through him now, but there was no denying its presence or its overwhelming strength. Staring down at the blond-haired woman in his bed, he silently made her a promise. No matter what it took, he would do everything in his power to keep her and their child safe and healthy.

"Where's Cactus?" Melissa asked when she came downstairs to find Shane sitting at the computer in his office.

"He and a couple of the men who stayed around for the weekend are playing poker down at the bunkhouse," Shane answered, looking up from the screen.

"What excuse did you give him about my...sudden exit from the room?" She could only imagine what the outspoken old man had to say about that.

"He didn't ask," Shane said, shaking his head. "He muttered something about it being my fault he burned the bacon as he scraped your plate into the garbage disposal." He shrugged. "I didn't bother to correct him." His expression changed to one of concern. "Are you feeling all right?"

His consideration touched her deeply. She had awakened to find a plate of crackers and a cup of weak tea on the bedside table, along with a note from him, telling her not to get up until she had consumed both. Apparently Shane had found the home remedy on the Internet, and whether it had been the nap or the crackers and tea, she did feel a lot better.

Nodding, she sat down in one of the two leather armchairs in front of his desk. "Right now I'm doing fine. I don't know for certain, but I assume since it's called 'morning sickness' that I won't be bothered again until tomorrow when I wake up."

"Good." He stood up and walked around the desk to sit in the chair beside her. "I've been checking the Web for information on pregnancy and doctors. If the tea and crackers work to help alleviate the worst of the nausea, it's best to stick with that, rather than a prescription medication. I'll set my alarm to get up earlier and have them waiting on you when you wake up tomorrow."

She smiled. "It sounds like you've done quite a bit of research."

"You wouldn't believe how much information there is on pregnancy." Clearly amazed, he shook his head. "The first thing we need to do is make an appointment with an obstetrician and get you on prenatal vitamins. Then, we'll have to review your diet to see where nutritional adjustments are needed."

Melissa stared at him a moment as she tried to assimilate Shane the ladies' man, with Shane the expectant father. "I intend to call for an appointment as soon as you take me back to Aspen," she assured him. "And I'm certain I'll be given instructions on what foods I should avoid and what I should add to my diet, when I see the doctor."

Nodding his obvious approval, he went on. "We'll also need to—"

She held up her hand to stop him. "Back up, Cowboy. Where is all this 'we' stuff coming from?"

"I told you, angel. I'm going to be with you every step of the way." He reached over to take her hand in his. "You're not going through this alone."

"I truly appreciate your willingness to help," she said slowly. "But if I'm in California and you're here in Colorado—"

"That's unacceptable," he interrupted, shaking his head. "I'm not going to let you risk losing your inheritance, Lissa."

"And I can't take the risk of having even one of the investors pull out of the upcoming projects planned for Jarrod Ridge."

Unable to sit still, Melissa rose to her feet to pace the floor in front of his drafting table. They had reached the moment she had been dreading. Decisions were going to be made that would affect the rest of their lives, as well as that of their child's. She just hoped with all of her heart they made the right choices.

"There are a lot of people dependent on the resort's success." She needed to make him understand. "Jarrod Ridge is the single largest employer in Aspen. If future projects like the Food and Wine Gala are canceled because the investment capital isn't there, people will start losing their jobs."

"None of that is going to happen," he said calmly.

Turning to face him, she couldn't believe his assertion. "You know Elmer Madison and Clara Buchanan. They are huge investors in Jarrod Ridge and two of the most puritanical members of the group, not to mention the most influential. We both know they'd disapprove of me becoming an unwed mother and convince several of the other investors to take their money elsewhere. I can't be responsible for—"

"The first thing I want you to do is calm down," he cut in. "Stress isn't good for you or the baby." His commanding tone indicated that the issue wasn't up for debate. "And the second is, you're worrying for nothing. Once they learn we're getting married, there's nothing they can say without looking like the pompous, judgmental asses they are."

"Shane—"

"Hear me out, Lissa." He rose to his feet, then walked over to loosely wrap his arms around her waist. "There's no way I'm going to allow you to go back to California to have our baby alone."

"You're starting to sound like a bully again," she warned. No one had told her what she was or wasn't going to do since she had left home after high-school graduation, and she wasn't inclined to let Shane pick up where her father had left off.

"I'm not being a bully. I'm trying to get you to see reason." His tone was less dictatorial and he had apparently gotten the message that she wasn't going to be ordered around. "This is my child, too, Lissa. We may not have planned on you becoming pregnant, but that doesn't mean I don't want to be just as much a part of his life as you do."

She had always wanted children some day and prayed that their father would be more interested and involved than her own father had been with his. That would be next to impossible with her living in one state and Shane in another.

Nibbling on her lower lip, she shook her head. "I'm sure we could work something out that gives us both equal time."

"Don't you see? Marrying me solves everything, angel." He drew her close to press a kiss to her temple. "You get to keep your inheritance, the resort keeps its investors and our baby gets a full-time momma and daddy to raise him."

Either her resistance was down or what he said was beginning to make sense to her. She did want to maintain her share of Jarrod Ridge and she could likely only do that by remaining in Aspen to manage Tranquility Spa. If she married Shane, some of the investors might grumble about her becoming pregnant before the marriage, but it should be enough to keep them from pulling their funding.

Leaning back, she gazed up at his handsome face. She had always hoped to have a husband and family, but in her dreams she had imagined marrying for love, not to save the resort's reputation and funding.

He must have sensed her resolve was weakening. "I give you my word that you won't regret becoming my wife, Lissa," he promised. "We can make this work. We already have a lot more going for us than other couples have."

His statement took her by surprise. "We do?"

He nodded. "We get along well, we enjoy and appreciate some of the same things, we have a fantastic love life and a baby on the way. The way I see it, that's a damned fine start."

"But there's still a lot we don't know about each other," she said, unwilling to give in so easily.

"We'll learn as we go," he said with a knowing grin.

The skunk knew she was going to agree with his plan. Was it too much to ask that he not gloat about it?

"How would we tell everyone the news?" she asked, wondering what her family would say.

Shane looked thoughtful for a moment. "I can make reservations to throw a dinner party in the Sky Lounge. I'm a Jarrod Ridge investor and given the way your family feels about losing its backers, I'm sure your brothers, sister and their significant others will feel compelled to attend."

If there was one thing she was certain of, it was the compliance of her family with one of the resort's investors. Shane and his father before him had contributed quite a lot of money to special events at

Jarrod Ridge. There was no way her brothers would risk losing that.

"I can't think of a single reason that anyone in my family would turn down your invitation."

"Good." His grin widened. "Now, can you think of anything else we should do before we tell your family?"

She shook her head. "Not at the moment."

"Then there's only one thing left to do." He dropped to one knee and taking her hand in his, smiled up at her. "Melissa Jarrod, would you do me the honor of becoming my wife?"

Staring down at Shane, she couldn't help but wonder what she was getting herself into. "I can't believe I'm about to say this," she murmured. Closing her eyes, she took a deep breath. Then, straightening her shoulders, she opened her eyes and nodded. "Yes, Shane, I'll marry you."

Six

The following week as he sat thumbing through a magazine in the obstetrician's waiting room, Shane took note of the pregnant women around him. Their stomachs were various sizes, and he couldn't help but wonder what Lissa would look like in the months to come.

Tossing the magazine on a table beside his chair, he glanced over at her, sitting beside him. He tried to envision her slender figure growing large with his child. From his research, he had learned that some women didn't start showing their condition until late in the pregnancy, while others blossomed early. He wondered which way Lissa would carry their baby.

His speculation was cut short when a nurse called

their names. "Melissa and Shane, if you'll follow me, we'll get your blood work taken care of and weigh you before the doctor does your examination."

Once the woman had drawn Lissa's blood and collected what she needed for a variety of other tests, they were ushered into a small room at the end of the hall. Taking both of their health histories, the nurse finally gave Lissa instructions on preparing for the examination and left the room.

"I think they know more about me now than I do," Lissa said as he helped her lay back on the uncomfortable-looking table.

"If you stick with the same doctor, they'll have all the information on record and it won't take as long the next time," he said, seating himself in a chair beside her.

Raising up on one elbow, she looked at him as if he had sprouted horns and a tail and carried a pitchfork. "Next time?"

"Well, I assumed you'd want more than one child," he said, wondering what the hell had gotten into him. They were just at the beginning of one pregnancy and he was talking about another?

If someone had told him a week ago that he would be sitting in a doctor's office, waiting to find out when his baby was due, he would have laughed them into the next state. Now, he found himself looking forward to learning the approximate time he would become a daddy and discussing the possibility of even more children.

Unreal.

"Let's get me through this pregnancy first," she advised, lying back down against a pillow. "Then we'll discuss our options."

He was saved from opening his mouth and making things worse with her when an attractive middle-aged woman, wearing a set of scrubs and a lab coat, walked into the room. "I'm Dr. Fowler," she said, smiling.

For the next half hour, the doctor examined Lissa, told them what to expect during the first trimester and answered their questions. Then, giving them an approximate date in April for the birth, she handed them a list of do's and don'ts and told them to make an appointment to see her in a month.

"I think I'm on information overload," Shane said as he escorted Lissa across the clinic parking lot to his truck. He helped her up into the cab, then walked around to the driver's side and slid in behind the steering wheel. "What do you say we go to the ranch and chill out until the dinner party tomorrow night?"

"That sounds good," she said, buckling the shoulder belt. "I don't particularly want to run into any of my family until after we tell them our news."

"Why not?" he asked, starting the truck. Never having had a brother or sister, sibling dynamics were something of a mystery to him.

"My brothers probably haven't noticed my frequent absences from the spa this week, but I know my sister, Erica, and my brother's fiancée, Avery, have." She shook her head. "They're sure to ask why I canceled our lunch date today, and I don't want to lie to them."

"I don't blame you." He liked that she was honest and preferred not to say anything, rather than tell a lie.

"Have you told Cactus anything about all of this?" she asked, hiding a yawn behind her delicate hand. "I'm sure he's curious."

Shaking his head, Shane turned the truck onto the road heading west out of Aspen. "No, but he has to know something is up."

"Has he said anything?"

"Not a word."

"Then how do you know he's aware there's something going on?" She looked bewildered and so darned cute, it was all he could do to keep from stopping the truck in the middle of the road and kissing her senseless.

"I've never brought a woman to the ranch before," he answered.

"Never?"

Shane shook his head. "Nope."

"So that's why Cactus was so surprised to see me that morning," she said, sounding sleepy.

"Yup. He hadn't seen a woman in that house since my aunt and her family left Aspen to move to Santa Fe."

He wasn't sure why, but he had never before felt

compelled to bring a woman home with him. Nor had he ever been tempted to take a woman to see Rainbow Falls. At least he hadn't until he met Lissa.

Glancing over at her, he realized she had fallen asleep. What was it about her that was different from other women he had been involved with?

As he steered the truck onto the private road leading over the ridge to the ranch, Shane decided that he was probably better off not knowing. There were some questions that were better left unanswered and he had a feeling this was one of them.

"Melissa, you look amazing," Avery Lancaster said, when she and Melissa's brother Guy walked up to her outside of the doors to the Sky Lounge. "Is there a new facial treatment in the spa I haven't heard about?"

Hugging her brother's fiancée, Melissa smiled as she shook her head. "I've just been getting more rest and eating a bit healthier."

It wasn't a lie. Of late, all she wanted to do was sleep and she had added an extra serving of fruits and vegetables to her diet each day.

"Well, whatever you're doing is working," Avery said, laughing. "You're positively glowing."

"You do look different," Guy agreed, frowning.

The fact that her brother thought he noticed a change in her was a bit of a shock. Since meeting the beautiful wine expert at his side, he was barely aware of anything else around him.

Melissa's brother Trevor chose that moment to stroll over to them. "Do any of you know what this party is all about? I've never known McDermott to be overly social. Usually the guest lists for his get-togethers consist of himself and the lady of the moment."

"Are you sure you aren't talking about yourself?" Guy asked, grinning.

Unrepentant, Trevor laughed. "I never said I thought McDermott was in the wrong on that."

"To answer your question, I have no idea what this dinner is about," Guy said, opening the door to the lounge. When the three went inside, he held the door for Melissa. "Are you coming?"

"I'll be there in a minute," she said, spotting her half sister, Erica, and her fiancé, Christian Hanford, as they got off the elevator.

Listening to her family speculate about Shane's invitation was the last thing she needed. Her nerves were already as tight as a bowstring. Once they made their announcement about getting married and having a baby, the course would be set. She just prayed with everything that was in her it was the right one.

"Avery and I missed you at lunch yesterday," Erica said, hugging Melissa close. "Are you all right?"

Feeling guilty for avoiding her newfound sister for the past week, she nodded. "I'm fine. I've just been preoccupied lately with…a new project."

Melissa truly liked her half sister and regretted that her father hadn't let them all know about her.

But whatever Donald Jarrod's reasoning had been, the family hadn't learned of her existence until the reading of their father's will two months earlier.

"Let's go in and see what McDermott has up his sleeve," Guy's twin, Blake, suggested as he joined them. As usual Blake had his trusted secretary, Samantha Thompson, at his side, and Melissa wondered for at least the hundredth time since meeting her how long it would take for Blake to realize what a beautiful woman Samantha was.

As the five of them entered the Sky Lounge, Melissa immediately spotted Shane at the doorway of one of the private gathering rooms, greeting her family as they arrived. He always looked good to her, but tonight he looked positively devastating in his black suit and tie. Very few men could look at ease in business suits as well as jeans and a work shirt. Shane managed to do it effortlessly.

"Where's Gavin?" he asked when they reached him.

"He should be here shortly," Blake answered, shrugging. "As we were getting on the elevator, I saw him in the lobby, talking to an old friend of his."

Motioning toward a large round table in the center of the room, Shane smiled congenially. "Have a seat and we'll get started as soon as he gets here." Trailing behind the two couples, Melissa stopped when Shane touched her arm. "I want you to sit in one of the two chairs tipped up against the table," he whispered close to her ear.

Seeing the chairs with their backs leaning against the table's edge, she nodded. Walking over, she set the chair upright and seated herself. She knew from the look on Erica's face that her sister expected Melissa to sit in the empty chair beside her. She hated that she might have hurt Erica's feelings, but she was sure her sister would understand once she and Shane explained the purpose of the party.

"Sorry I'm late," Gavin apologized as he and Shane approached the table together. "I ran into one of the guys we graduated high school with and stopped to say hello."

Once her brother was seated with the rest of her family, Shane straightened the chair beside her, but instead of seating himself, he remained standing. "I know you're all wondering why I invited you here tonight," he said, making eye contact and smiling at each individual at the table.

"Well, now that you mention it, we did—" When his oldest brother elbowed him, Trevor stopped short to glare at Blake.

Shane smiled. "I don't blame you. I would have been curious, too, Trevor."

Melissa tightly clenched her hands, resting in her lap. He was about to reveal the secret they'd kept for the past two months, and although it would be a relief to have their affair out in the open, she just hoped they were doing the right thing.

Lost in thought, she was surprised when Shane reached down to take her hand in his and pull her up to stand beside him. "Since your sister's return to Aspen a few months ago, we've been seeing each other and our relationship—"

"I knew it!" Trevor said triumphantly. Obviously proud of himself for noticing what the others had missed, he added, "When I saw the two of you together back in July, I knew something was going on."

"Don't break your arm patting yourself on the back there, Trevor," Gavin said drily. "I suspected Melissa was hiding something, too. I just didn't know what it was."

When the laughter at the table died down, Shane put his arm around Melissa's shoulders and gazing into her eyes, announced, "Lissa and I wanted all of you to be the first to know, we're getting married and will be welcoming our first child next spring."

Before anyone could react, Shane lowered his head and gave her a kiss that caused her head to spin and her toes to curl inside her sensible black pumps. When he finally raised his head, there was a hushed silence. Then, everyone started talking at once.

"Congratulations you two," Guy said, grinning from ear to ear. "It looks like my pastry chef is going to be busy for quite some time making nothing but wedding cakes."

"That's great," Trevor said happily. "Now that McDermott is off the market, I won't have as much competition with the ladies."

"I'm so happy for you," Erica said, rushing around the table to hug Melissa.

Avery was right behind Erica to wrap her arms around Melissa. "I never suspected a thing. I don't know how you managed to keep quiet about a relationship as serious as this." Giving her a watery smile, Avery added, "I think it's wonderful."

As her brothers and Christian took turns shaking Shane's hand, Melissa noticed that although Blake's secretary, Samantha, added her congratulations, the woman seemed uncharacteristically quiet and subdued. What could possibly have the vibrant brunette so down in the dumps?

Before she had a chance to speak to the woman and ask if everything was all right, Gavin wrapped Melissa in a brotherly bear hug. "I wish you every happiness, little sister."

Tapping on his water glass with the edge of his knife, Blake drew everyone's attention. "I'd like to make a toast."

To her surprise, one of her brothers had ordered a bottle of champagne and the waiter had just poured them all a glass of the sparkling pink wine. All except for her and Avery. Their glasses held sparkling white grape juice.

"I'm pregnant," Melissa said, pointing to Avery's glass. "What's your excuse?"

Her friend made a face. "Remember, champagne makes me sneeze."

Melissa didn't have time to dwell on the matter when Blake raised his glass.

"To Melissa and Shane," he said, smiling. "May you have a long and happy life together.

Everyone raised their glass in agreement, then taking a sip of wine, settled down to dinner and conversation. As it always did, talk turned to plans for expanding the resort's services and special promotions. Melissa tuned most of it out as she watched her family.

Apparently so did Erica and Avery. They'd been huddled together since finishing their desserts and she wondered what the two of them were up to.

All in all, the evening had gone quite well, she decided, feeling more at ease than she had in several days. It was a huge relief to have her and Shane's relationship out in the open.

As the evening drew to a close and everyone gathered their things to leave, Erica and Avery pulled Melissa aside. "Let's get together for lunch on Wednesday," Avery said, her eyes twinkling.

"We want to start making plans for a baby shower," Erica added, just as excited.

Melissa was touched by their enthusiasm and happiness for her. "I'd like that, but don't you think it's a bit early to start planning something like that? I'm only a couple of months along."

"You can never start planning the perfect party too early," Avery said, laughing.

"Besides, from everything I've been told, it will

start getting extremely busy in a couple of months when the ski season starts," Erica agreed. "If we get most of the details worked out now, we won't be so rushed later on."

Agreeing on a time for their lunch, Melissa watched her sister and future sister-in-law leave the restaurant. She loved finally having female family members. After growing up as the only girl in a house full of boys, it was definitely a welcome change.

"I think everything went pretty well tonight," Shane said, walking up to put his arm around her. "At least, none of your brothers threatened to grab their shotguns and run me out of town."

She laughed. "I doubt that any of them own a shotgun." As they walked from the Sky Lounge, she added, "I'm just glad everything is out in the open and we don't have to sneak around anymore."

"Yeah, I'm not going to miss those midnight treks from the stables through the woods to Willow Lodge one damned bit. It's a wonder someone hadn't noticed and thought I was a Peeping Tom." Waiting for the elevator, his laughter turned into a grin that held such promise it stole her breath. "From now on, I'll just roll over and turn out the light."

"Really?" she asked, laughing at his lascivious grin.

"Most definitely." He leaned close to whisper, "And just in case you have any doubts about that, I intend to give you a demonstration as soon as we get back to the lodge."

* * *

Using Lissa's key, Shane let them into Willow Lodge, then closing and locking the door behind them, took her into his arms. He nibbled kisses from her neck up to her delicate earlobe.

"I've been wanting to have you all to myself all evening." Used to being alone with her, he'd had the devil of a time keeping his hands to himself.

"The dinner party did seem to drag on, didn't it?" She put her arms around his waist and snuggled close. "Thank you, Shane."

He leaned back to gaze down at her. "For what?"

"For taking charge tonight when we told my family about us." She kissed his chin. "I wasn't quite sure how to go about it."

"I never said I hadn't rehearsed a few dozen different speeches before I settled on one." He grinned. "When you're in a room full of men who just might take your head off and shout down your neck because you got their little sister pregnant, it inspires you to think things through."

"You did just fine," she said, unknotting his necktie. He loved the feel of her fingers brushing his throat as she removed the silk tie.

Placing his hands on her shoulders, he turned her around. "As good as you look in this dress, I think you'll look much better out of it."

Slowly sliding the zipper down from her neck to her lower back, he sucked in a sharp breath. "Good thing I didn't know earlier that you weren't wearing a bra," he said, kissing the back of her neck. "I'd have never made it through the evening."

When he started to slide the black dress from her shoulders, she caught the front to her and shaking her head, stepped away from him. "Why don't you build a fire in the fireplace while I change?"

As she walked from the room, Shane blew out a frustrated breath and slipping off his suit coat, unbuttoned and rolled up the sleeves of his dress shirt. Building a fire hadn't been high on the list of things he'd had planned for the evening. In fact, it hadn't been anywhere on it. But it was something Lissa wanted, and he was finding more and more that he was willing to do whatever it took to make her happy and see her pretty smile.

A nice fire had just started crackling in the stone fireplace when the lights in the great room went out. A moment later, Lissa walked up and knelt down beside him in front of the hearth.

"I thought these might be nice to snuggle up with," she said, setting a stack of pillows and a couple of fluffy blankets on the floor beside him.

Glancing over at her, he did a double take. She was wearing the sexiest black satin robe he had ever seen. One side of the slinky little number had slipped down over her bare shoulder and he knew as surely as he knew his own name, she didn't have a stitch of clothes on beneath it.

"Do you want me to make some hot cocoa?" she asked before he could find his voice.

Shane swallowed hard and shook his head. The shimmering light cast by the fire seemed to bathe her in gold, and he knew for certain he had never seen her look more beautiful.

"The only thing I want is right here beside me," he said, pulling her to him. He brushed his mouth over hers. "Do you have any idea how sexy and desirable you are?"

"I haven't really thought about it," she said, toying with the top button of his shirt. "I've been too busy thinking about how much I think you deserve a good, relaxing massage."

His mouth went as dry as a desert in a drought. What man in his right mind would turn down having a beautiful woman run her hands over every inch of his body?

Without a word he stood up, and while she arranged the blankets and pillows on the hardwood floor in front of the fireplace, he made short work of taking off his clothes. It was only after he lay facedown on the soft blankets that she slipped the robe off. Dropping it beside him, she picked up a bottle of oil that he hadn't noticed before. He felt her pour several drops of the warm liquid onto the middle of his back.

At the first touch of Lissa's palms on his bare skin, Shane felt as if he had died and gone to heaven. Her gentle, soothing touch was driving him crazy and his reaction was not only completely predictable, it was immediate.

By the time she worked her way down the back of his thighs and calves, then told him to turn over, he felt as if the temperature in the room had gone up several degrees. Never in his entire life had he experienced anything as exciting and arousing as having Lissa's hands gliding over his body.

Their eyes met and, holding his gaze with hers, she drizzled a small amount of the oil onto the middle of his abdomen. As she caressed his shoulders and pectoral muscles, Shane ached with the need to hold her, to touch and excite her as she was doing to him.

"Enough," he said, catching her hands in his to pull her down beside him.

Covering her mouth with his, he traced her soft lips with his tongue. He didn't think he had ever tasted anything sweeter. When he coaxed her to open for him and the tip of her tongue touched his, he felt as if a charge of electric current coursed from the top of his head all the way to his feet.

He broke the kiss and turned her to her back. Deciding to treat her to a little of the same sweet torture she had put him through, he picked up the bottle of oil. Smoothing the slick liquid over her satiny skin, he paid special attention to her breasts and tightly puckered nipples. By the time he moved down to her flat stomach, he wasn't certain which one of them was suffering more.

The blood rushing through his veins caused his ears to ring as he stared down at her. Her expressive blue eyes reflected the same hunger that filled him and her porcelain cheeks wore the blush of intense passion. Shane knew for certain he would remember her this way for the rest of his life.

The evidence of her desire fueled his own and the need to once again make her his was overwhelming. Using his knee to part her thighs, he settled himself over her.

"P-please," she murmured.

"What do you want, angel?"

"You." She reached to put her arms around him. "I want you, Shane."

His breath lodged in his lungs as he pressed himself forward and her supple body accepted him. Closing his eyes for a moment in a desperate attempt to hang on to his rapidly slipping control, he held himself completely still. He wanted to make this last, to love her slowly and thoroughly. But when she wrapped her long legs around his hips to hold him to her, Shane knew he had lost the battle.

With his pulse pounding in his ears like a sultry jungle drum, he slowly began to rock against her. The way she met him stroke for stroke, their bodies perfectly in tune, sent a flash fire to every fiber of his being and clouded his mind to anything but the mind-blowing pleasure surrounding them.

All too quickly, he felt her body tighten around his. Her feminine muscles clung to him, driving Shane over the edge, and he felt as if he had found the other half of himself when together they found the release they both sought.

Melissa couldn't help but smile when she snuggled against the man sleeping next to her. After they made love in front of the fireplace, he had carried her into the bedroom to make love to her again. Then, true to his word, he had rolled over and turning off the bedside lamp, pulled her close and gone to sleep.

As she studied his handsome face, she thought about how wonderful he had been at dinner. He had seemed genuinely happy when he told her family about their upcoming marriage and the baby they'd have in the spring.

Placing her hand on her still-flat stomach, she couldn't help but marvel at the fact that she was going to be a mother. For as long as she could remember, she had hoped to one day have a precious little miracle of her own to hold and love. She reached out to touch Shane's strong jaw with her fingertip. He had made that happen and she couldn't help but love him for it.

Her heart skipped a beat. She had known from the beginning of their affair that she was in danger of getting in over her head. He had been clear that their involvement was temporary and she had wanted that, too. But the attraction she had felt for him was too strong, had been too immediate not to pose a serious threat to her peace of mind.

She had told herself she could control her infatuation and avoid falling in love with him as long as she kept things in perspective. She knew now that she had been lying to herself all along.

If the truth was known, she had fallen in love with him the moment they laid eyes on each other two months ago. He was the most charming, considerate man she had ever met and the longer she was around him the deeper her feelings had grown.

Her chest tightened and a tear slid down her cheek. She quickly swiped it away with the back of her hand. In the coming months, she was going to have almost everything she had always hoped for. She was going to marry the man she loved, have a home in one of the most beautiful places on earth and start the family she had always longed for.

So why couldn't she be happy and content with that?

Melissa knew exactly what was keeping her picture-perfect fantasy from becoming reality. She wanted it all. She wanted the home, the family and the one thing she wasn't sure Shane would ever be able to give her…his love.

Seven

"It looks like I'll just have to take a couple of the appointments myself," Melissa said as she and Rita went over the afternoon reservations.

"I'm so sorry, Ms. Jarrod," Rita apologized for at least the tenth time. "I don't know how I could have made that kind of mistake."

"It's all right, Rita. These kinds of things happen from time to time," Melissa assured her. "Just look a little closer next time to make sure there's an opening at the time requested by the guest."

Rita was beginning to gain more confidence and improve her managerial skills, and Melissa was hopeful that would continue. She knew the woman was a single mother and needed the job to support herself and her son. She certainly didn't want to cause Rita any more stress by having to replace her.

"Ready to go?"

Looking up, Melissa smiled at Avery as she entered the Tranquility Spa's reception area. "Would you mind if we have lunch in the Sky Lounge today?" she asked. "I only have an hour or so before I have to be back."

"Problems?" Avery asked.

Giving Rita an encouraging smile, Melissa shook her head. "Not really. I'm afraid there was a mix-up and we're overbooked this afternoon. It seems all of the Jarrod Ridge guests want a spa treatment before this weekend's dinner honoring the investors. I'm going to have to do a couple of the massages and at least one of the facials myself."

"Wow! You are busy," Avery said, her eyes widening. "But that actually works out better for me, too." She grinned. "In fact, I was going to ask you if the Sky Lounge would be okay. I wanted to stop by and talk to Guy for a few minutes after we eat."

"What about Erica?" Melissa asked, grabbing her purse. "Is she going to be able to meet us?"

Avery nodded. "I called her this morning and asked her to get a table by one of the windows and that we'd meet her in—" she looked at her watch "—oops. Five minutes ago."

"Then I suppose we'd better get going," Melissa said, laughing. She loved that in the past couple of months she had gained a sister and a future sister-in-law that were also quickly becoming her best friends.

A few minutes later, as they got off the elevator and entered the Sky Lounge, they immediately spotted Erica and hurried over to the table she had been saving.

"I'm sorry we're running late," Melissa apologized as she slid into one of the empty chairs.

"You can blame me for that," Avery said, seating herself. "Guy was running late leaving to go to the restaurant this morning because I…that is we…I mean—"

Grinning as they watched Avery squirm, Melissa and Erica both propped one elbow on the table, cupped their chins in their hands and asked in unison, "Yes?"

"Uh, never mind." Avery's cheeks were pink as she shook her head and quickly picked up a menu. "I think I'm going to have the tuna melt."

"Nice save," Melissa said, laughing as she picked up her menu.

After they placed their order, the conversation turned to plans for the baby shower. "I won't know for a few more months whether to decorate in pink or blue," Melissa said, shrugging.

Erica smiled. "What are you hoping for? A boy or a girl?"

"I haven't really given it much thought," Melissa admitted. "But it doesn't matter to me as long as the baby is healthy."

"That's all that's important," Avery said, nodding.

Choosing a date in February for the shower, they discussed nursery themes and shops where Melissa should register. By the time they finished lunch and left the restaurant, she had only a few minutes to get back to the spa.

"I suppose I'll see you both on Saturday evening at the dinner?" she asked as they got off the elevator in the lobby.

"Christian and I wouldn't miss it," Erica said.

"We'll be there." Avery grinned. "I'll probably have a hard time keeping Guy out of the kitchen, though. You know how he is about wanting every dish to be perfect."

"Since Guy took over managing the resort's restaurants and brought in Louis Leclere as chef, the efficiency of the kitchen staff has improved greatly," Melissa said.

"The new items they've added to the menu seem to be a big hit, too," Erica added.

Melissa checked her watch. She had only a few minutes to make it to the first massage appointment. "I'm really sorry, but I have to run. See you on Saturday."

As she hugged them both and headed down the hall toward the spa entrance, something Erica asked her at lunch kept running through her mind. It didn't matter to her whether their baby was a boy or a girl.

But did it matter to Shane whether they had a son or a daughter?

Like most men, he would probably prefer to have a boy. But she didn't think he would be disappointed either way. Unfortunately, it was hard for some men to hide their feelings. She had always suspected that her father had been disappointed she was female.

Of course, she couldn't say he had treated her brothers much better. He had driven all of his children to be overachievers and in the process alienated them from the very thing he had wanted them to embrace—Jarrod Ridge.

Shaking her head, she relegated thoughts of her late father to the back of her mind as she walked through the reception area of Tranquility Spa and prepared to go back to work. The sooner she finished for the day, the sooner she and Shane could leave for the ranch.

For some reason he had insisted they have dinner at Rainbow Bend, which was fine with her. She loved the peace and quiet of the remote ranch and after a day filled with booking mix-ups, Melissa couldn't wait to get there.

"Dinner was delicious, Cactus," Lissa said as she helped clear the table. "How did you know I love country-fried steak smothered in milk gravy?"

The elderly man beamed. "I didn't, but I sure am glad you liked it, gal."

Shane sat back and watched the exchange with

interest. Cactus didn't care for most people and the fact that he was falling all over himself to please Lissa said a lot. If Shane didn't know better, he would swear the old boy was completely smitten.

Of course, he couldn't blame Cactus. With each passing day, Shane found himself thinking about her more often, wondering what she was doing and counting the hours until they could be together again. It was something he wasn't sure he was comfortable with, but there didn't seem to be anything he could do to stop it, either.

Deciding that it would be better for his peace of mind to simply not think about it, he left the table. "Lissa, I have something that I'd like for you to take a look at."

"Can it wait?" she asked, handing Cactus a plate to rinse. "After that wonderful meal, the least I can do is help Cactus with the cleanup."

"Don't you worry about it, gal," Cactus said, shaking his head. "Since Shane got me this here dishwasher, I don't mind doin' kitchen chores near like I used to."

"Are you sure?" When Cactus nodded, she surprised the old man by kissing his wrinkled cheek. "Thank you for dinner. It was wonderful."

Shane had known Cactus all of his life and he'd never known the man to be at a loss for words. He always had something to say, whether it was to give his unwavering opinion or complain—which was usually the case. But the old geezer couldn't seem to find his voice. He just stood there wearing the sappiest expression Shane had ever seen.

"You wanted to show me something?" Lissa asked, drawing Shane's attention. She had walked over to him and he had been so astounded by Cactus's atypical behavior, he hadn't noticed.

Smiling at her, Shane nodded. "But there is something I think we need to do first."

"What's that?"

"We are going to make Cactus's day," he whispered close to her ear. Shane put his arm around her shoulders and tucked her to his side. "Cactus, what would you say if I told you that pretty soon you'll be able to cook for Lissa a lot more?"

"That'd suit me just fine," Cactus said, nodding his approval. "She's a danged sight more appreciative 'bout my cookin' than you are."

Shane laughed. "So you want me to start kissing you now after every meal?"

"Try it and you'll be missin' your front teeth," Cactus warned, turning back to the dishes in the sink.

"Then I guess after we get married, I'll just have to leave the kissing up to Lissa," he said, anticipating the old gent's reaction. Shane didn't have long to wait.

He hadn't seen Cactus move as fast in years as when he spun around to face them. "Well, I'll be damned." If he'd had teeth, his ear-to-ear grin would have lit a city block. "Married, you say?"

Shane glanced down at Lissa and winked. "Do you think I should tell him the rest?"

"You might as well," she said, smiling.

"There's going to be a baby joining us in the spring." A sudden, unfamiliar feeling settled in his chest and Shane realized that he was actually beginning to get excited by the prospect of becoming a daddy.

"I guess now that there's gonna be a woman and youngin' underfoot, you're gonna expect me to stop my cussin', scratchin' and spittin'," Cactus said, his grin belying his complaint.

"It probably wouldn't be a bad idea." Laughing, Shane turned Lissa toward the hall, then called over his shoulder, "You'll have to give up cooking breakfast in your long johns, too."

As they walked down the hall to his study, he chuckled. He could still hear Cactus grumbling about kids, women and bone-headed ranchers who expected him to give up everything worth doing.

"What did you want to show me?" Lissa asked, when they entered the study and he closed the door.

She looked so sweet and desirable, he didn't think twice about taking her into his arms and kissing her until they both gasped for breath. When he finally raised his head, Shane drew in some much-needed air.

"I've been wanting to do that all day."

Her smile sent his temperature skyrocketing. "I've missed you, too."

"How was your day at the spa?" he asked, a bit surprised that something so mundane suddenly felt important to him.

She shook her head. "Don't ask. You really don't want to know."

Leaning back, he frowned. "That bad, huh?"

"Just tiring." She explained about the booking mix-up, then smiling, asked, "How about you? Anything interesting happen?"

"I got a call from Sheik Al Kahara." He shrugged. "He wants to hire me to design all new stables for the Thoroughbred farm he just bought in Kentucky."

"That sounds like a challenge," she said, sounding genuinely interested. "Do you have to do a lot of traveling with jobs like that?"

"I have to travel occasionally, but not more than once or twice a year." He shook his head. "Most of my clients e-mail the size of stable they want and what they want included in the design. I send them a quote and then once we sign the contracts, I go to work on the design. But the sheik's is going to be a piece of cake. He basically wants the same setup I designed for the stables at his palace in Almarif."

Her eyes widened. "Do you have a lot of foreign clients?"

"I have quite a few."

"Are they all royalty?"

Her curiosity about his career pleased him more

than he would have thought. "Not all of them are royalty, but I have designed stables for several members of this or that monarchy." Taking her hand, he led her over to the other side of the room. "But I don't want to talk about sheiks or stable designs right now." He motioned for her to sit in one of the chairs in front of the fireplace. "I want your opinion on something."

"I can't guarantee how much help I'll be, but I'll try," she said, smiling as she settled into the high-backed leather armchair.

"Oh, I think your opinion on this counts for a lot more than you think." He turned to remove the small, black velvet box he had placed on the fireplace mantel before leaving to pick her up after she got off work. Flipping the box open, he turned to hold it out to her as he watched for her reaction to the pear-shaped diamond solitaire in a white-gold setting that he had bought for her the day before. "Do you think you would be interested in wearing this to the investors' dinner on Saturday evening?"

If the look on her face was any indication, he had hit a home run. "My God, Shane, it's beautiful."

Removing the sparkling jewelry from the box, he took her left hand in his to slip the ring on her third finger. To her delight and his relief, it fit perfectly.

"How did you know my ring size?" she asked, jumping from the chair to throw her arms around his neck.

"I guesstimated," he said, catching her to him. "So you like it?"

"I love it." She leaned back to stare down at her hand. "It's exactly what I would have chosen." Then, looking up, the smile she gave him lit the darkest corners of his soul. "Thank you."

"Are you ready for my other surprise?" he asked, kissing the tip of her nose. He decided there wasn't anything he wouldn't do just to see her smile at him like she was at that very moment.

Her eyes widened. "There's something else?"

He took her by the hand and led her out of the study to the front door. "I want you to close your eyes and keep them closed until I tell you to open them."

"What are you up to now?" she asked, laughing.

"If I told you it wouldn't be a surprise." Shane grinned. "Would you rather I blindfold you?"

She shook her head. "No, I promise I'll keep my eyes closed."

Once she did as he asked, he helped her down the porch steps and across the yard. "Don't peek," he warned, releasing her hand to untie a set of reins from the corral fence.

"Shane, what on earth—"

Placing the leather straps in her hand, he said, "Okay, you can open your eyes."

When she did, she looked puzzled. "I don't understand."

"Stormy is yours now, angel." The look on her face was everything he had hoped for.

"He's mine?" Her eyes sparkled as she stared at the blue roan, standing saddled in front of her.

"Yup." Shane grinned. "I've already sent in the paperwork to transfer his registration to you."

She glanced at the sun sinking low in the Western sky. "Do you think we have enough time to take a short ride?"

Grinning, Shane nodded. "I thought you might want to do that. That's why I had one of my men saddle Stormy and have him ready." As Lissa mounted her horse, Shane walked into the stable. He returned with his stallion and swung up onto the saddle. "We should have time to ride to the trailhead that leads to Rainbow Falls and make it back before dark."

"Thank you for everything." Riding the roan up beside his sorrel, Lissa leaned over to kiss his cheek. "This is the nicest, most thoughtful thing anyone has ever done for me." Her delighted expression suddenly turned to a teasing grin. "You are going to get so lucky tonight."

"Then let's get the hell out of here," he said, nudging his stallion into a lope.

"What's your hurry, Cowboy?" she asked, laughing as she urged Stormy to follow.

"I want to get back." When she caught up to him, he grinned. "I could really use some…luck."

* * *

As they rode across the valley back to the stable, Melissa couldn't keep from smiling. "I love it here."

"Really?" It sounded as if Shane had a hard time believing she meant what she said.

"Who wouldn't love this?" Twisting around in the saddle, she took in the majestic beauty of the surrounding snowcapped mountains. "This has to be the quietest, most peaceful place on earth."

"Some people would rather live where there are people around and things to do besides sit and listen to the grass grow," he said, staring straight ahead.

She shook her head. "I'm not one of them."

"That reminds me. There's something else we need to discuss before we get married," he said slowly. "Where do you want to live?"

Confused, she stopped her horse. "This is your home. I assumed you'd want us to live here."

Reining in the stallion, Shane turned to meet her questioning gaze. "I do want to live here. It's home. But I also know and accept that once the snows start, I may only get out of the valley a handful of times until the spring thaw. I accept the fact that there isn't a convenience store just around the corner. It's a good ten-mile drive if you forget to buy something while you're in town."

It was almost as if he was trying to talk her out of living on the ranch. Once they were married, didn't he want her to live with him?

"I remember you telling me the first day you brought me here that the road leading into the valley sometimes gets closed off for several weeks."

His intense gaze caught and held hers. "Do you think you can stand being snowbound for that long?"

She stared at him for several moments before she spoke. "I can't answer that right now because I've never been in that situation, Shane." She flicked the reins to urge Stormy into a slow walk. "What I can tell you is this. I understand all the drawbacks of living here and I'm still more than willing to give it a try."

Each lost in thought, neither had much to say as they rode into the ranch yard. Dismounting the horses, by the time they had the animals groomed and turned into their stalls, Lissa had started yawning.

"I have to send an e-mail to a potential client. Why don't you go on upstairs and take a hot shower?" Shane asked, when they entered the house. He caught her to him for a quick kiss. "I promise I won't be long."

"I think I'll do that," she said, hiding another yawn. She smiled apologetically. "I'm beat."

"I know, angel." Kissing her again, he released her and took a step back. "I'll be up in a few minutes."

Shane watched her climb the stairs before he went into his study and opened his e-mail. Quickly composing a message with a quote for his architectural services, he pressed the send button, then turning off the computer, sat back in his desk chair.

The evening couldn't have gone more perfectly. Lissa had loved the engagement ring he'd bought her and couldn't have been happier when he gave her the roan gelding. The ride to the trailhead had gone well, too—right up until she mentioned how much she enjoyed the peace and quiet of his ranch.

What had gotten into him anyway? Why couldn't he have taken her at her word that she wanted to live on the ranch? Why had he felt compelled to point out all the drawbacks of living on the Rainbow Bend?

Something he had overheard his father tell Cactus right after Shane's mother left kept running through his mind. At first, Carolyn McDermott had loved living on the ranch and hadn't minded the isolation. But as the years went by, being snowbound for weeks on end and having no neighbors close by had taken its toll and she had come to hate the picturesque valley.

After living on the ranch for a while, would Lissa end up feeling the same way? Would her resentment grow to the point that she left and never looked back?

Unlike his mother, Lissa was from Aspen and well aware of what the weather was like in the Rocky Mountains. But she had lived in California for the past eight years and although she said she missed the winter activities, she also liked living on the beach. After being snowbound a few times, what if she decided she preferred the more temperate climate of Malibu? And what if instead of leaving her child behind as his mother had done, Lissa took their son with her?

Staring at the dark computer screen, Shane drew in a deep breath. He didn't think Lissa would do that to him. Even before he'd convinced her to let him do the honorable thing and make her his wife, she had told him that arrangements could be made for him to be part of their child's life.

Rising from the chair, he turned off the desk lamp and left the study to head upstairs. Lissa had told him she wanted to try living on the ranch and that was really all he could ask of her. Only time would tell if her enthusiasm would turn to loathing. As long as he kept that possibility in mind and didn't allow his fondness for her to develop into a deeper emotion, he should be fine.

Unfortunately, he was finding that harder to keep in check with each passing day. Lissa was quickly becoming an addiction, and one that he wasn't sure he would ever be able to live without.

Eight

"How was your meeting with the other Jarrod Ridge investors this afternoon?" Melissa asked when Shane stopped by the spa the following afternoon.

"Long and boring as hell." He chuckled. "At least it was right up until I made my little announcement about our engagement." Laughing out loud, he shook his head. "You should have seen Elmer Madison's and Clara Buchanan's faces."

"Let's go into my office and you can tell me all about it," she suggested, not wanting to talk in front of the spa staff and resort guests.

They had agreed that he would tell the other members of the investment group they were getting married, but decided to wait until after the wedding to let them know about the pregnancy.

Once they entered her office and closed the door, she turned to face him. "Tell me what happened."

"When Elmer asked if there was any more business we needed to discuss, I stood up and announced that I'd asked you to marry me and that you had said yes."

He took off his cowboy hat and sailed it over to land on the couch. Then, pulling her against him, he kissed her until she saw stars.

"I—I want…details," she said, trying to catch her breath when he finally lifted his head. "What could they possibly find wrong with our getting married? You didn't mention the baby, did you?"

"No, that would have probably sent both of them into outer space." Shane shook his head. "I think they are both scared to death that, by marrying you, I'll get in on an investment they won't."

"That's ridiculous." She frowned. "All investments for special events are done through the group. They can pull out of the group at any time or choose not to support a project, but we offer all investment promotions to the group as a whole, not to individuals."

"I know, angel." He shrugged. "It might be they are afraid that once I'm married to you, I'll start contributing more and end up getting a bigger return on my money. Either that or they're both a few cards shy of a full deck." He grinned. "My guess is it's a little of both."

"Did they say anything?" She couldn't imagine what it would be if they had.

"Nope. They didn't say a word."

"Then how do you know they had a problem with our getting married?" Maybe Shane had misinterpreted their reaction.

His blue eyes twinkled with humor. "When I said that you and I were getting married, old Elmer turned so red in the face, I thought he might bust that blood vessel that stands out on his forehead whenever he gets upset."

"What about Clara?" Melissa asked, trying not to laugh at the visual picture Shane was painting. "What was her reaction?"

"She was taking a drink of water and got so choked, I thought I was going to have to perform CPR on her." He made a face. "I'd rather climb a barbed-wire fence buck naked than put my mouth on hers."

"And all this time, I thought you had a secret crush on Clara," she teased.

His exaggerated shudder and horrified expression had her laughing so hard, she found it hard to breathe. "Not in this lifetime. Just the thought of getting 'cozy' with that old bat is enough to make a man swear off women for good."

She couldn't stop laughing. Clara was at least twice Shane's age and always looked as if she had just sucked on a lemon.

His expression suddenly turned serious. "Lissa,

I want you to know that although the pregnancy brought about our decision to get married, you don't have to worry. I give you my word that I'll always be a good provider and a faithful husband."

Taken aback by his unexpected proclamation, she stared at him. "I'll be a good, faithful wife to you. But what brought this on?"

"I know that my reputation of moving from one woman to the next is only slightly better than Trevor's," he explained. "I just wanted you to know that I honor my commitments. You never have to worry about me going out and finding someone else."

After spending so much time with him in the past couple of weeks and seeing him interact with Cactus, she knew for certain Shane wasn't that kind of man. "It never crossed my mind that you wouldn't be anything but faithful to our marriage."

The sudden knock on the door came as no surprise. The spa had been extremely busy all day with guests getting ready for the dinner tomorrow night.

Reluctantly leaving Shane's arms, Lissa walked over to open the door. "Is there a problem, Rita?"

"I hate to bother you, but Joanie just got sick and had to go home," her assistant manager explained. "She has two half-hour facials booked and I'm afraid all of the other girls' schedules are full. Will you be available to take her place or should I cancel the appointments?"

"I'll be right there, Rita." When the woman went

back to the reception desk, Melissa closed the door and turned to Shane. "I'm really sorry, but I have to get back to work. We've really been slammed today. It looks as if I'm not going to get out of here for at least another couple of hours."

He picked up his hat from the couch and walked over to where she stood by the door. "I need to go anyway." He gave her a tender kiss, then reached for the doorknob. "I have to pick up my tux at the cleaners and then I have a couple of things Cactus wanted me to get before we go back to the ranch for dinner." Shane grinned. "He's planning on making you his world-class beef stew and sour-dough biscuits."

Just the thought made her mouth water. "That sounds scrumptious."

Nodding, Shane opened the door. "I'll be back to pick you up this evening around five."

Walking out into the reception area, Melissa sighed as she watched Shane leave. She loved him and if she hadn't known that before, she would have after his reassurance that he would be a good husband.

Cowboys had a reputation for their word being their bond. If it was important enough for him to tell her he would be committed to their marriage, then he fully intended for it to work out between them.

It hadn't been the declaration of love she would have preferred, but it was enough to give her hope. Maybe one day he would say the three words she longed to hear.

* * *

"When would you like to get married? Shane asked as he and Lissa sat in front of the Willow Lodge fireplace. After having dinner with Cactus, he had driven them back to the cabin for a nice quiet evening alone in front of a crackling fire.

"So much has happened over the past couple of weeks, I haven't had time to give it a lot of thought," she said, snuggling against him. "But I'd like to wait until after Erica and Christian's wedding. I don't want to take anything away from their special day."

He nodded. "I can understand that. When is it?"

"Christmas Eve." She looked thoughtful for a moment. "What would you think of a New Year's Eve wedding?"

"Sounds good to me," he said, kissing the top of her head. "Do you want a big wedding?"

"Not really." She sat forward and reached for her mug of hot cocoa. "I think I'd like something small with just family and close friends."

"Whatever you want, angel." He grinned as he leaned over to kiss away a smudge of melted marshmallow from the corner of her mouth. "I guess the next question would be where do you want the ceremony?"

He watched her look around the great room of the lodge. "I think right here would be nice."

"You don't want to get married at Jarrod Manor?" He'd thought she would want to have it at the family mansion.

"No." Her emphatic answer surprised him.

They stared at each other for several silent moments before he asked, "Why not, Lissa?"

She hesitated, then just when he thought she was going to avoid answering his question, she shook her head. "I don't have a lot of pleasant memories there."

"But that's where you grew up." He reached for her cup of cocoa to set it on the coffee table, then took her hands in his. "What was there about it that made you unhappy, angel?"

"There wasn't any one thing," she said, sighing. "It just never felt like much of a home to me."

"Why is that?"

He watched her shrug one slender shoulder before she met his questioning gaze. "I think you've probably figured out by now that I wasn't overly close with my father."

Shane nodded. From what she'd said about her dad wanting his children to start learning about the resort at such an early age and her obsession with how other people's opinions of her could reflect badly on Jarrod Ridge, he'd come to the conclusion that Donald Jarrod had placed his business above all else and taught his children to do the same.

"I've been told that when my mother was alive my father wasn't as focused on Jarrod Ridge as he became after her passing," she said quietly. "But for as long as I can remember, he never had time for us. He was always too busy either working or traveling to promote the resort." Her expression turned resentful. "And he expected us to make Jarrod Ridge our number-one priority, as well."

He had dealt with Donald Jarrod on several occasions through the investors group, as well as when the man bought horses for the resort stables, and he didn't think he'd ever met a bigger workaholic. But surely Jarrod had realized his family was more important than business.

"Maybe he was unaware—"

"Oh, I think he knew." She rose from the couch to walk over to the floor-to-ceiling windows of the great room. "Unfortunately, it's too late now to do anything about repairing our relationship."

Shane got up from the couch to walk up behind her. Wrapping his arms around her, he pulled her back against him. "I'm sure your dad was just trying to be a good provider for you and your brothers, angel."

She sighed. "That might be, but tell that to a child wanting nothing more from her father than his love and attention."

Although Shane's dad had lost interest in almost everything in life after his wife left, he'd still been there to raise his son. And, in his own way, Shane was certain his father had loved him. But apparently Lissa hadn't had that assurance.

"You at least had your brothers," he said, tightening his arms around her.

Nodding, she rested the back of her head against his shoulder. "I did, but they were all older. Besides, they were boys and didn't want to play with dolls or have tea parties."

Shane chuckled. "No, I can't imagine any of your brothers wanting to do that."

She turned within the circle of his arms to face him. "Just the thought is pretty amusing, isn't it?" she asked, the ghost of a smile curving her coral lips.

He nodded. "Blake would have probably shown up in a suit and tie and Trevor would have invariably brought a date."

Her smile broke through. "Of course."

Happy to see that her mood had lightened considerably, Shane pressed his lips to hers. "So it's decided, then. We'll get married here on New Year's Eve with family and close friends."

Resting her head against his chest, she nodded. "I think I'm going to invite Hector and Michael. They're two of my closest friends in Malibu, and besides, I'd like to talk to them about running the spa for me with the option to buy after a specified length of time."

"Are you sure you want to get rid of your business?" It pleased him that she intended to make her move to Colorado permanent, but he hated to see her give up a business she'd built from the ground up and was obviously quite proud of.

"It's not so much that I want to get rid of it," she admitted, yawning. "But I grew up with a father who was more absent than not and I don't want that for our child from either of his parents. Besides, I'll have

Tranquility Spa, and if we stay as busy as we are now, I'm going to talk to Blake about expanding."

"Uh-oh. It looks like the sandman is about to pay you a visit," he said, chuckling when she yawned again. "We had better get you to bed."

"I hope I can stay awake during the investors' dinner tomorrow evening," she said when he rose and guided her toward the hall.

"Yeah, it would be a shame to fall asleep during one of the speeches." Shane laughed.

"Maybe I better plan on taking a nap tomorrow afternoon," she said as they entered the bedroom.

"I'll plan to take one with you," he said, giving her a wicked grin.

"You're insatiable, Mr. McDermott," she said, shaking her head.

He took a step toward her. "And I intend to show you just how ravenous I am as soon as we get into bed."

As he and Lissa walked into the Jarrod Ridge Grand Ballroom for the festivities, Shane knew beyond a shadow of doubt that he was with the sexiest, most beautiful woman in attendance. Lissa had put her long blond hair up in some kind of soft, feminine twist, exposing her slender neck. He would like nothing more than to kiss every inch of it.

But the long, shimmery black evening dress she wore was what had his libido shifting into high gear. Slinky and form-fitting, it emphasized every one of her delightful curves and each time she moved it reminded him of a sleek jungle cat's elegance and grace.

Remembering where they were, he tried to rein in his unruly hormones. If he didn't get things under control soon, everyone in the whole damned place would know exactly what he had on his mind.

He spotted Clara Buchanan on the other side of the room and concentrated on how she would react to the evidence of his wayward thoughts. That was enough to take the wind out of any man's sails.

"There's Blake and his secretary, Samantha," Lissa said, bringing him back to reality. "They'll be seated at the head table with Erica and the rest of my brothers."

"What about us?" he asked. "Is that where we're sitting?"

"No. As an investor, you'll have your own table and I told Guy to have the kitchen staff put my place card next to yours."

"You're both looking very nice tonight," Trevor said, walking up to them. Lissa's brother had a pretty, young brunette clinging to his arm.

"Good to see you again," Shane said, shaking Trevor's hand.

After a few minutes of exchanging small talk, Trevor and his date moved on. "I wish he would settle down a bit," Lissa said quietly. "I've seen Elmer and Clara watching him, and they don't look all that pleased."

Putting his arm around her bare shoulders, Shane kissed her temple. "I agree that your brother is known to play it pretty fast and loose with the ladies, but it's really none of Elmer's or Clara's business what he does or how he chooses to conduct his life."

Before Lissa could respond, several of the regular resort guests came over to greet them and pay their compliments to Lissa's family on another spectacular event.

"The food in past years has been very good, but the cuisine this year is outstanding," George Sanders, a food critic from Los Angeles, said enthusiastically. "As soon as I find him, I intend to let Guy know the resort's pursuit of culinary excellence will be the focus of my next column. The crème brûlée is to die for."

"I'm sure Guy will be very pleased to hear that," Lissa said, smiling.

Once the portly gentleman stopped gushing about the food and moved on, Shane placed his hand on Lissa's back. "Why don't we find our table and see who our dinner partners are?"

He could use a reprieve and he was sure Lissa felt the same way. Besides, hearing himself repeat the same greeting at least twenty times, his face felt as if it had frozen in a permanent grin.

When they found their table close to the main table at the front of the room, Shane held Lissa's chair, then settled himself onto the one beside her. "It looks like we're hosting the politicians," he said, glancing at the place cards on the elegantly set table.

She nodded. "I just hope they put their political differences on hold for the evening."

"I'll see what I can do about that," Shane offered. "I happen to know that Senator Kurk and Representative Delacorte are both into fly-fishing. If it looks like the conversation is going to turn into a debate, I'll invite them both to go fishing next spring on the Rainbow."

"Thank you," she said, looking grateful. "I would really like for the evening to remain free of controversy."

"Shane, my boy, I hoped I would see you here this evening," Senator Kurk said, approaching their table. "I think you know my wife, Beatrice?"

Shane stood up while the older woman sat down. "It's nice seeing you again, Mrs. Kurk," he said nodding. He shook the senator's hand, then sat back down. "I'm glad you could join us."

"The way I hear it, congratulations are in order. A little bird told me you're planning on taking a trip down the aisle," the man said, smiling at Lissa. "Is this lovely girl your bride-to-be?"

"Senator Kurk, Mrs. Kurk, I would like for you to meet my fiancée, Melissa Jarrod," Shane introduced them.

"Melissa?" Beatrice Kurk exclaimed, disbelievingly. "I didn't recognize you, dear. You're all grown up. I think the last time we saw you, you were getting ready to leave for college."

As Lissa and the senator's wife exchanged pleasantries and caught up, Representative Delacorte and his wife arrived. Dinner was served shortly afterward and to Shane's immense relief, the two politicians seemed to have put their opposing political views aside for the evening.

While the women asked Lissa about new services at the spa and plans for their upcoming wedding, Shane found himself enjoying the men's stories of fishing for trout in the various rivers and streams in the Rocky Mountains. He was even surprised to learn the men were pretty good friends when they weren't at loggerheads over political issues.

As they waited for dessert to be served, the two men and their wives politely excused themselves. Shane knew they were going to work the room and try to secure votes for the upcoming elections before the event's closing speeches began.

Relieved to once again be alone with her, Shane turned to Lissa. But her attention was trained on her brother Trevor seated at the head table with her other siblings and their respective dinner companions.

"I can't believe what he's doing," she said, shaking her head. Seated beside a shapely redhead, the brunette that had been clinging to Trevor earlier was nowhere in sight. "I can only imagine what Elmer and Clara are thinking right now."

Watching his future brother-in-law whisper something to the redhead, then while her head was turned, wink at a blonde seated a few tables to the left of the head table, Shane had to admit the man was asking for a boatload of trouble. He saw nothing wrong with a single man playing the field. Hell, he'd had his own share of women before he met Lissa. But Shane had at least had the good sense to limit himself to being with one woman a night.

If Trevor wasn't careful, he was going to set himself up to be right in the middle of a class-A catfight. And once the women figured out he'd been playing all of them, they would stop blaming each other and turn on him with claws bared.

"Shane, could I speak with you in private for a moment?" Senator Kurk asked, standing at Shane's shoulder. Engrossed in the show at the head table, he hadn't seen the man approach.

"Of course," Shane answered, somewhat puzzled by the senator's serious demeanor. Rising from the table, he kissed Lissa's cheek. "I'll only be a few minutes."

He hated leaving her alone, but relieved to see Avery Lancaster heading toward their table, Shane turned his full attention to the man walking beside him. He had never seen Patrick Kurk look as serious or as determined as he did at that moment.

When Avery sat down in the chair next to her, Melissa couldn't help noticing the scene playing out just beyond her friend's shoulder. Her brothers Guy and Gavin had walked up behind Trevor at the head table. One of them spoke to him, then all three men left the room.

"What's going on?" she asked, turning to her friend.

"Guy and Gavin are going to strongly suggest that Trevor use a little more discretion with the female guests here tonight," Avery answered quietly.

"I'm glad," Melissa said, meaning it. "He's not doing the resort's reputation any favors."

"You mean 'come to Jarrod Ridge and get your heart broken by one of its handsome owners' isn't going to be the resort's new slogan?" Avery asked sardonically.

Melissa loved Avery's quick wit. "I somehow doubt that would help business," she said, laughing.

"Where's Shane?" Avery asked, looking around.

"Senator Kurk wanted to speak to him in private about something." Unconcerned, Melissa took a sip of her water. "He's probably hitting Shane up for a campaign donation or wants him to volunteer to hold some kind of fundraiser."

Avery nodded. "It's not enough that politicians want our vote, they also want our money."

"Are Guy and Gavin having their talk with Trevor?" Erica asked as she joined them.

Melissa smiled at her sister. "I'd say it's hitting the fan, even as we speak."

Erica winced. "I'd hate to be in poor Trevor's shoes right now."

"Me, too," Melissa and Avery both spoke at the same time.

"I'm glad I have you two together," Melissa said, deciding it was time for a change of subject. Even though Trevor deserved getting the warning about his notorious behavior, she took no pleasure in it having to be done. "One of the guests at the spa left a magazine in the reception area and it had pictures of a nursery decorated with an 'under the sea' theme," she explained. "I really liked it and I think that's what I want to use for the nursery. It incorporated all of the pastel colors and had the cutest baby sea creatures."

"I looked at that just the other day," Avery said, nodding. "It's adorable."

Melissa briefly wondered why Avery had been looking at nursery themes, but dismissed the thought. Her friend had probably been looking for ideas to use for the baby shower.

"I love the little pink sea horse and blue octopus," Melissa added, knowing she had settled on the theme she wanted for the nursery.

"It would be perfect for a boy or girl, too," Erica agreed enthusiastically. "And we can use all of the colors when we decorate for the shower."

Melissa hugged both women. "You two are the best. Thank you for planning this baby shower for me."

"Uh-oh. It looks like I'm going to have to go soothe the savage beast," Avery said suddenly, pointing toward Guy as he walked back into the ballroom.

"He doesn't look as if the encounter with Trevor was pleasant."

"I doubt that it was," Melissa said, hating that her family had to deal with yet another conflict.

"I'm afraid I need to get back to Christian," Erica apologized, rising to her feet. "I see he's been cornered by someone, no doubt looking for free legal advice."

As she watched her two best friends walk back to their fiancés, Melissa wondered where Shane was. She checked her watch. He had told her he would only be a few minutes and that had been a half hour ago.

Deciding he would probably be back soon, she left the table to freshen up before the closing speech began. As she started down the hall toward the ladies' powder room, she couldn't help but recognize Shane's voice coming from just around the corner.

"I'm flattered that you asked me to help with the investigation, Senator," Shane said. Melissa started to join him and the senator, but his next words stopped her in her tracks. "I have a couple of stables to design, but after I send the blueprints to the contractors, I'll have all the time in the world to devote to the investigation."

"There could be times when you'll have to do some frequent traveling," Senator Kurk warned.

There wasn't even so much as a moment's hesitation before Shane answered the man. "That won't be a problem. There's nothing keeping me from spending all the time needed on the job sites and giving them my undivided attention."

Lissa couldn't stand to hear any more. She and their child were nothing? Hadn't he listened to what she'd told him just the night before?

Feeling as if her heart had shattered into a million pieces, she turned and walked straight to the resort's lobby. Shane was no different than her father had been. He intended to put work ahead of his family, and that was something she just couldn't accept.

At the front desk, she asked for a piece of the resort's letterhead and an envelope. When she finished scribbling the note, she sealed it in the envelope and handed it to one of the clerks working the reservations desk.

"I want this delivered to Erica Prentice at the head table in the Grand Ballroom," she said, surprised that her voice sounded so steady. "Take it now before the closing speech starts."

"Yes, Ms. Jarrod," the young woman behind the counter said. "I'll take it to her right away."

As the woman hurried down the corridor leading to the ballroom, Melissa thought about walking to the lodge, but decided against it. She had left her light wrap at the table and the temperature outside had already dropped considerably. Besides, she didn't relish the idea of walking that distance in three-inch heels.

She turned to the concierge. "I want someone to drive me to Willow Lodge."

The man nodded. "It may take a few minutes to—"

"Now!" If she didn't get back to the lodge soon, there was a very real danger of her falling apart right there in the middle of the lobby.

Never having heard her bark orders at anyone, the man moved faster than she had ever seen him and in no time Melissa found herself seated in the back of one of the resort's courtesy limousines. She forced herself to remain stoic on the short ride up the road to Willow Lodge. She knew that she had already caused enough gossip and speculation among the employees with her outburst at the concierge. She didn't want to add more by dissolving into a sobbing heap in the back of the limo.

When the driver stopped in front of the lodge, she got out and hurriedly let herself inside. Only after she had closed and locked the door did she give in to the emotions that she had held in check since overhearing Shane and Senator Kurk.

First one tear and then another slipped down her cheeks and Melissa rushed into the bedroom to collapse on the bed. As she stared at the diamond ring on her left hand the loneliness of a lifetime came crashing down on top of her. She had never been able to live up to her father's expectations and it appeared that she wasn't enough for Shane now.

Nine

When Shane and the senator returned to the ball-room the closing speech had just begun and all eyes were focused on Blake Jarrod, Lissa's brother, the new CEO of Jarrod Ridge. As he thanked the guests and investors, Shane looked around for Lissa.

Where the hell had she gone? Had she become ill and had to leave? If so, why hadn't she found him to take her back to Willow Lodge?

As he scanned the crowd to see if she might be sitting at another table, he glanced at the head table. Lissa's sister, Erica, was staring at him and he could tell from her expression that she knew something about where Lissa might be.

Frustrated by the fact that he couldn't get to

Erica to ask where Lissa had gone until after Blake concluded his speech, Shane barely heard his name being called when the investors were asked to stand and be recognized. By the time Blake gave his closing remarks, Shane was already on his feet and threading his way through the crowd to the head table.

"Where did Lissa go?" he demanded when he reached Erica.

"Just before Blake's speech she sent me a message that she was having someone take her back to Willow Lodge," Erica said, looking worried. "Do you think she's not feeling well?"

"I don't know, but I'm sure as hell going to find out," he said, already turning toward the door. "Thanks."

"Please let me know if she's all right," Erica called after him.

Nodding that he would, Shane impatiently made his way through the crush of people leaving the ballroom. Was there something wrong with her or the baby?

As all of the things that could go wrong during the first trimester ran through his mind, he quickly decided that he'd done a little too much research about pregnancy. Apparently, ignorance really was bliss. It had to be better than the hell his imagination was putting him through now.

It seemed as if it took an eternity to make his way across the crowded lobby and out the resort's main doors. Unwilling to wait for the valet to bring his truck around, Shane broke into a run as he headed for the lane leading up to the private lodges.

Why had Lissa sent her sister the message saying she was leaving instead of him? What had happened between the time he and the senator stepped out into the corridor and the time they reentered the ballroom?

As he sprinted up the steps and across the deck of Willow Lodge, he fished for the key Lissa had given him from his pocket. His fingers felt clumsy as he rushed to unlock the door and let himself in.

"Lissa?" he called when he finally opened the door.

The silence was deafening. He glanced around the room. Her handbag was lying on the couch as if she'd tossed it aside so he knew she was there.

"Lissa, where are you?" he called, his heart thumping against his ribs as his fear increased. When he found her in the bedroom, she was lying on the bed, sobbing uncontrollably. "Lissa, angel, what's wrong?"

Before he could sit on the side of the bed and take her into his arms, she raised her face from the pillow she clutched. "D-don't, Shane." Shaking her head, she scooted to the opposite side of the mattress. "P-please just...go home."

What had gotten into her? When he left the table at the dinner, she had been fine.

"What's wrong?" he demanded.

"I want you…to leave," she sobbed. "Just go… back to your ranch…and leave me alone."

"Angel, you're not making sense," he said, trying to maintain a patient tone. "Calm down and tell me what happened to make you so upset."

Pushing herself to a sitting position, she swiped at her eyes with the back of her hand, then shook her head. "I overheard you and Senator Kurk."

"And?" He couldn't think of a single thing they had discussed that would send her into such an emotional meltdown.

"There's nothing to keep you from traveling extensively?" She shook her head. "What about me? What about our baby? Are we always going to come in a distant second to whatever project you're working on? Aren't we important enough to you that you want to be with us?"

"Calm down, Lissa."

"Don't tell me what to do, Shane. All my life I've come in last place behind a man's work and I won't do it again." Her eyes flashed with a mixture of hurt and anger. "Answer my question. Do you or do you not want to be here with me to make a marriage between us work?"

He had told the senator he was free to travel and devote his time to investigating design flaws in several federal and military buildings. But he couldn't tell her the reason he'd agreed, because he didn't like admitting—even to himself—that he needed distance to regain his perspective.

When he remained silent, Lissa's crushed expression caused his gut to twist into a painful knot. "I think your silence is answer enough, Shane." Removing the engagement ring he had given her, she reached across the bed to place it in his hand. "I'm just glad we discovered that it wouldn't work out between us before we actually got married."

"Lissa—"

"Don't, Shane," she said, sounding completely defeated. "There's really nothing left to say."

Staring at her for several long moments as he tried to put his tangled thoughts into some semblance of order, he shook his head. "This isn't over, Lissa."

Silent tears slid down her smooth cheeks. "Yes, it is, Shane."

He could tell from the look on her face she wouldn't listen to anything he had to say, even if he had been able to explain himself. "What about the investors and your family? What are you going to tell them?"

"That's really no longer any of your concern," she said flatly. "I'll handle whatever announcement I need to make regarding our breakup."

Suddenly angry, he asked, "What about the baby? I want to know—"

"From now on, anything you have to say to me can be done through Christian Hanford. Closer to the baby's birth, I'll have him contact your attorney to work out a custody agreement." She took a deep breath and pointed toward the door. "I'd really like to be alone now, Shane. Please lock the door as you leave."

He stared at her for a moment longer before turning to walk out of the bedroom. Placing the door key she'd given him on the kitchen counter, he let himself out of the house and descended the porch steps.

As he slowly walked down the lane toward the resort's main building, the engagement ring he still held felt as if it burned a hole in his palm. When he'd given it to her, he could tell it meant the world to her and he'd suspected then that she'd fallen in love with him.

He knew now that his instincts had been right on the mark. Lissa did love him and he could tell that it had broken her heart when she'd taken off the ring and handed it back to him only minutes ago.

His anger escalated, but it wasn't directed at anyone but himself. What the hell was wrong with him? How had he let things get so out of control?

He'd known for the past couple of weeks that he was walking a fine line, and keeping his feelings for Lissa in check was going to take monumental effort on his part. That's why he'd eagerly agreed to accept Senator Kurk's offer. He'd suddenly needed the distance between them to pull back before he found himself in far deeper than he'd ever intended to go.

But was it already too late? Had he done the unthinkable and fallen in love with her?

Shaking his head, Shane wasn't sure. And until he

got it all figured out, it would be best to leave things as they were between them. He'd already hurt her terribly. He'd rather give up his own life than do it again.

Standing on the deck at Willow Lodge, Melissa stared at the mountains beyond. How could her life have changed so dramatically, yet everything around her stayed the same? She had never experienced such emotional pain, never felt so alone as she did at that moment, yet the birds still sang and the sun still shone on the golden aspens whispering in the crisp mountain breeze.

Why had she deluded herself into thinking that Shane would be as committed to making their marriage work as she intended to be? How was it possible that she had missed seeing he was as driven by ambition and work as her father had been?

Shane had told her he would be faithful, and she had no doubt he'd meant what he said. But fidelity was one thing. Spending the time together that a couple needed to make a marriage work was something else entirely.

She had been willing to give up the life she'd built for herself in Malibu to remain in Colorado so that they could be a family. Was it too much to ask that he make a few concessions, as well?

The night he'd given her the engagement ring, he'd told her that his career required only occasional travel. But at the first opportunity that had come along for him to spend more time away from her and their child, he hadn't been able to agree fast enough.

All her life she'd come in a distant second to her father's ambition to make Jarrod Ridge the number-one resort in the Rockies. She refused to settle for second place with her husband.

"Melissa, is everything okay?" Turning at the sound of her sister's voice, Melissa watched Erica climb the steps and walk across the deck toward her. "You left the dinner so suddenly yesterday evening, I was afraid you might not be feeling well. Are you all right?"

"No, and I'm not sure I ever will be again," she said honestly. "But I'll survive. I always do."

"What's wrong?" Erica asked, clearly alarmed. "Are you feeling ill? It isn't anything with the baby, is it?"

Melissa shook her head. "As far as I know the baby is fine."

Erica looked around. "Where's Shane?"

"I don't know. Probably at his ranch." Since learning she had a half sister and welcoming Erica to the family, the two of them had grown fairly close and Melissa did need to talk to someone. "I broke off our engagement last night."

"Oh, no!" Erica immediately wrapped her arms around Melissa. "I'm so sorry. You both seemed so happy."

Melissa shrugged one shoulder. "It's probably

better that it happened now instead of after we got married."

"That's true," Erica agreed. "But it's still so sad." When the breeze picked up, she suggested, "Why don't we go inside and I'll make us both a cup of herbal tea?"

A few minutes later Melissa sat at the table, staring at the steam rising from the mug Erica had placed in front of her.

"Are you sure the two of you can't work things out?" Erica asked quietly.

"I don't see how." Over the course of the longest, loneliest night of her life, she had asked herself a thousand times if she'd made the right decision. Each time the answer had been that she had. "We both saw our relationship differently and I'm not sure that could ever change."

They were silent for several minutes before Erica asked, "Is there anything I can do?"

Melissa nodded. "You can be there for me when I let the rest of the family know the marriage is off."

"You know that Avery and I will both be there to support you no matter what," her sister said without hesitation. "For that matter, I can't imagine any of our brothers being anything but supportive."

"I hope so." Erica hadn't grown up in the same house with their father and therefore had no way of knowing how much emphasis had been placed on appearances and the family's reputation. "I've decided that I'll be going back to California soon.

I can have the baby out there without causing any disruption with the investors."

"Melissa, you can't do that. You'll lose your share of the resort." Erica shook her head. "No one wants to see that happen."

"If I don't, we could lose a considerable amount of funding for highly successful events like the Food and Wine Gala." She rubbed the tension building at her temples. "We've probably already lost one of our biggest investors."

Erica frowned. "Who's that?"

Melissa gave her sister a sad smile. "Shane."

"Do you really think he'll stop funding special promotions because the two of you are no longer involved?" Erica looked doubtful. "I'm sure he's made a lot of money from helping fund Jarrod Ridge projects. I wouldn't think he'd want to give that up."

"I don't know. It could be a bit uncomfortable for both of us." She took a sip of her tea. "But aside from Shane pulling out of upcoming projects, some of the others aren't going to look kindly on me being pregnant and single."

Erica touched Melissa's hand. "I think you're giving those people too much power over you. It's none of their concern what you do in your personal life."

"Shane said virtually the same thing," she admitted.

Maybe she was giving too much credence to what others thought of her family. But it was hard to cast aside a lifetime of instruction on the importance of others' opinions of her. For as long as she could remember her father had lectured his children on how their actions directly affected the resort and how important it was to protect Jarrod Ridge's reputation above all else.

"The main thing is you don't have to make a decision about any of this right away," Erica said, rising to place her cup in the sink. "You have plenty of time to weigh your options, then you can decide what *you* want to do."

After Erica left, Melissa sat at the table contemplating their conversation. In this day and age, many women chose to be single mothers and no one thought anything about it. So why was she afraid of what two busybodies had to say about her? And why was she willing to lose her inheritance because of it?

She wasn't. The only opinions that really mattered were those of her family. They loved each other and since their father's death the bonds between them were strengthening. Maybe her brothers would stand behind her and her decisions if she stayed in Aspen.

Sitting up straight, she came to a decision. She didn't care anymore what people like Elmer Madison and Clara Buchanan had to say about her becoming a single mother. They weren't living her life. She was.

If they pulled out of the investment group because of her pregnancy, it would be their loss. There were

probably several other townspeople who would readily take their place and reap the rewards of investing
in Jarrod Ridge. And if not, the family could pick up
the slack themselves.

Feeling slightly better, she sighed. If only she
could resolve her feelings for Shane that easily. But
making a rational choice to change your attitude
about something was far easier than trying to change
how you felt about a person.

There was no way around it and no way to stop
it. She loved Shane with every fiber of her being and
always would.

"Cactus, this is the worst meat loaf I've ever
tasted," Shane complained, pushing his plate away.

The truth was, the meal could have been prepared
by a gourmet chef and the results would have been
the same. Everything he'd tried to eat for the past few
days had tasted like an old piece of harness.

"It's been three days since you and that little gal
parted ways and I swear you're in a worse mood now
than you was when you first told me she wouldn't be
around no more," Cactus grumbled as he cleared the
dinner table.

Shane sighed and tuned Cactus out as the old
man continued his rant. He knew he was being unreasonable about everything with everybody. But
he couldn't seem to stop himself. He couldn't eat,
couldn't sleep and nothing he did seemed to relieve

the hollow ache that had settled in his chest when he walked away from Willow Lodge the other night.

"I'm sorry if I've been a little irritable," he said, knowing there was no excuse for taking out his bad mood on Cactus.

"A little irritable?" The old man looked disgusted. "Boy, I've seen pissed-off grizzly bears with better attitudes than yours."

Rubbing the tension at the base of his neck, Shane nodded. "I know. And I'm really sorry about that."

"Well, knowin' and doin' somethin' about it are two different things." Dishes clattered as Cactus dumped them into the sink. When he turned to face Shane, he pointed a wooden spoon at him. "Seems to me that if you're that miserable, you'd get your sorry hide back to town and see what you could do to patch things up with that gal."

"It's not that easy."

"Why ain't it?"

Shane wasn't surprised that Cactus thought it could be that easy. The old man saw things as black and white, right and wrong. If something went wrong, a person fixed it and moved forward. But some things just weren't that easy to repair.

"For one thing, I doubt that Lissa would open the door if I did go by her place."

"Then you catch her out somewhere and talk to her," Cactus shot back. "And if you have to get down on your hands and knees to tell her how sorry you are, then do it."

"How do you know I'm in the wrong?" Shane asked, feeling a bit affronted. He hadn't told the old man anything more than the wedding was off and Lissa wouldn't be visiting Rainbow Bend anymore.

"Far as women are concerned, it don't make no never mind who started it or what it's about," Cactus said sagely. "To their way of thinkin' it's always a man's fault."

"I'll take that under advisement," Shane said, starting down the hall. He didn't need to hear more of Cactus's advice on relationships. He already knew who was to blame for his and Lissa's breakup.

Once inside his study, Shane closed the door and walked over to his drafting table to sit down. He'd tried for the past couple of days to work on the plans for the sheik's stable, but hadn't accomplished a damned thing. For a man accused of being ambitious and driven, he certainly wasn't living up to expectations.

Staring off into space, he couldn't stop thinking about Lissa and the shattered look on her pretty face when he hadn't been able to answer her questions. He had a good idea he knew exactly why he had agreed to the senator's request to help with the investigation and it wasn't something he was proud of. Accepting the job had been his way of running, of trying to escape what he knew now to be inevitable.

He took a deep breath. A man never liked admitting, even to himself, that he was a coward. But the truth of the matter was, he was just plain scared.

Lissa made him feel too much. She made him want to reach out for the things that he had told himself he would never have.

Propping his elbows on the drafting table, Shane buried his head in his hands. Somehow when he wasn't looking, Lissa had gotten past his defenses and he'd done the unthinkable. He'd fallen in love with her.

His heart pounding in his chest like a jackhammer, he rose from the drafting table to walk over and stare out the window at Rainbow Valley. He hadn't wanted history to repeat itself, hadn't wanted to go through the same hell his father had by loving a woman.

But with the exception of trying to drink her memory away, Shane found himself in the same position. He loved Lissa and was finding it damned near impossible to live without her.

As he watched an eagle make a soaring sweep of the valley, he thought about something Lissa had said when she broke off their engagement. She felt she'd taken a backseat to a man's work all of her life. Now he was doing the same thing her father had done. From what he could remember, Donald Jarrod spent every waking minute overseeing every aspect of the thriving enterprise. And instead of the preferential treatment some men would have shown their own kids, Jarrod had seemed to expect his children to work harder and do more than anyone else.

It was no wonder when Lissa heard his conversation with Senator Kurk that she had assumed he was as driven and ambitious as her father. She had no way of knowing that he'd been running from himself and not striving to build his career.

He shook his head. Although he wanted to excel in his field, Shane had no intention of ever letting it take over his life. But he hadn't told her that the other night. Now, he wasn't sure she'd give him the chance.

But he had to try and he knew exactly where to start to make things right between them. Turning to walk over to his desk, Shane picked up the phone.

"Senator Kurk? This is Shane McDermott."

Ten

"Blake, is this a good time?" Melissa asked from the door of her brother's private office.

"What's up?" he asked, looking up from the papers on his desk that he and his assistant had been going over.

"There's something I need to tell you," she said, walking into the room.

"I'll leave the two of you alone," Samantha said as if sensing that Melissa's business with Blake was of a personal nature.

Of all of her brothers, Blake had turned out to be the most like their father. He was the consummate business man and had been the best choice to step in as CEO of Jarrod Ridge. He was also a bit intimidating.

Settling herself into the chair in front of his desk, she took a deep breath. "I wanted to let you know that I've ended my engagement to Shane."

His concerned expression when he got up and walked around the desk encouraged her. "I'm sorry to hear that, Melissa," he said, sitting down in the chair beside her. "Are you all right?"

The genuine concern she heard in his voice had her fighting back tears. "It's been a rough few days," she admitted. "But I'm doing okay."

"Is there anything I can do?" he asked.

"Not really." She shrugged one shoulder. "Although I'm sure once the word gets out around the resort there will be a lot of talk and speculation. I just thought you needed to know before that happens."

Blake nodded. "I appreciate that, but I'm more concerned about your welfare than I am the rumor mill."

"I hope you mean that, because I've made a decision I'm not entirely certain you'll be happy with." She met his puzzled gaze. "I'm staying here in Aspen."

His complete confusion was written all over his face. "Where else would you go?"

"At first I thought it might be best if I went back to California to have the baby." She stared down at her hands clasped tightly in her lap. Making the decision to place herself ahead of the resort was new to her and she only hoped her brother understood. "I know some of the investors aren't going to look favorably on my being a single mother, but—"

"I couldn't care less if those people contribute another penny to Jarrod Ridge," he interrupted.

Shocked at her brother's statement, she stared at him. "Really?"

He nodded. "They knew Dad would sell his own soul for this resort and its reputation. For years they've used that to hold us all hostage with the threat of withdrawing from the investors group. That ends now."

His decisive tone left no doubt in her mind that Blake meant what he said. "It won't make a difference if they do stop investing in special events, will it?" She didn't think it would, but she wanted to be sure.

Blake laughed. "Not hardly. Our great great-great-grandfather started the investors group when he needed capital to build Jarrod Ridge. We've grown way beyond needing anyone else's money to do whatever we want with the place."

"Then why hasn't the group been dissolved?" she asked, unable to understand why her father hadn't done so years ago.

"The same reason you were willing to give up your share of Jarrod Ridge and go back to California," Blake said. "Dad was afraid of what disgruntled investors like Clara and Elmer might say against the resort."

For the first time since walking into her brother's

office, Melissa felt some of her tension ease. "I take it you don't care what they say?"

"The locals aren't the ones keeping Jarrod Ridge going, nor do they make or break our reputation," he said, grinning as he shook his head. "The tourists do that. We keep the townspeople afloat with the clientele we bring in. I seriously doubt they're so vindictive they would bite the hand that feeds them."

"I hadn't thought of it like that." Rising, Melissa hugged her brother. "Thank you, Blake. Our talk has helped me more than you can imagine."

"That's what family is for, Melissa," he said, returning to sit at his desk. "And I'm sorry things didn't work out with you and McDermott."

"Me, too," she said sadly as she left his office.

As she walked back to the spa, Melissa wondered why her father hadn't seen what Blake pointed out about the resort's importance to the town. Or maybe he had and used the fear of ruining the resort's reputation to manipulate and control his children. Either way, the next generation of Jarrods weren't going to have to live under the threat of other people's opinions.

But the resolution to that problem brought little relief. In fact, it only gave her more time to think about Shane and the incredible loneliness and heartache she'd felt since breaking off their engagement.

Lost in thought, she was halfway across the reception area when she realized her assistant manager had called her name. "Is something wrong, Rita?" she asked, turning to face the woman.

"Ms. Jarrod, I'm afraid I've made another mistake with this afternoon's schedule," Rita said, looking as if she might burst into tears. "I don't know how it happened, but we have a guest in the Green Room, waiting for a massage and there isn't a masseuse available. Could you take the appointment?"

Sighing, Melissa nodded as she headed for the Green Room at the back of the spa. "Not a problem, Rita. Just double-check before you book next time."

In truth, she was glad to have something to take her mind off of how much she missed Shane. Anything was better than sitting in her office, thinking about all the things that could never be.

As soon as she opened the door to the dimly lit therapy room, the piped-in sound of a waterfall seemed to wash over her and caused her to catch her breath. She'd probably never be able to hear the sound again without thinking of Shane and the afternoon they'd spent together at Rainbow Falls.

Glancing at the massage table, she did a double take. There wasn't anyone there. The sound of the door being closed and the lock being secured had her spinning around to face whoever was in the room with her.

"Hello, Lissa." The male voice was so low, so warm and intimate, it felt as if he caressed her, and it caused her heart to skitter to a complete halt.

"Shane, what on earth do you think you're doing here?"

The sight of him was both heaven and hell rolled into one. She'd missed him so much, but the thought that they'd never be together caused such emotional pain, it was all she could do to keep from crying out from its intensity.

"I told you the other night that our discussion wasn't over," he said, advancing on her.

She quickly skirted the massage table to put it between them. "And I told you there wasn't anything left to say."

Wearing nothing but a towel wrapped around his waist, he folded his arms across his wide chest and shook his head. "Maybe you don't have anything more to add, but I have plenty."

Melissa closed her eyes and tried not to think about how wonderful it felt to be wrapped in those arms, to lay her head on that bare chest and have him hold her throughout the night. Opening her eyes, she shook her head. "Please, don't do this, Shane."

"Don't do what, Lissa?" he asked calmly. "Explain why I agreed to help Senator Kurk with the investigation? Or don't tell you about the war I've been waging with myself about why I hesitated to answer your questions?"

Why was he doing this to her? Couldn't he see it was tearing her apart just being in the same room with him and knowing they could never have a future together?

"None of it matters, Shane," she said, trying desperately to keep her voice from cracking. "You can't change, and I won't settle."

"Yes, it does matter, angel," he said, his deep baritone wrapping around her like a warm cloak.

Knowing that he wasn't going to leave her alone until she heard what he had to say, she pointed to his towel. "Do you really think this is the kind of conversation we should be having with you wearing nothing but that?"

"I don't have a problem with it." He moved his hand to release the terry cloth where it was tucked at his waist, causing her to go weak in the knees. "But I can take it off if you want me to."

"N-no," she said hastily, holding her hand up to stop him. "The towel will be fine. Just tell me what you came here to say, then leave."

He motioned toward the lounge chair in the corner. "This might take a while. Why don't you sit down?"

With her legs feeling as if they might not support her much longer, she conceded and walked over to lower herself onto the lounger. When he started to walk over to her, she shook her head. "You can say what you need to from over there."

If he got any closer there was a good chance he would reach out and touch her. That was something she couldn't allow to happen. If he did, she knew for certain she'd lose every ounce of her resolve.

She watched him take a deep breath. The movement of his rippling abdominal muscles sent a shaft of longing straight through her. Quickly averting her eyes, she concentrated on his suddenly serious expression.

"First of all, I want you to know that I'm not like your father, Lissa. I'm not driven to work every waking minute." He shook his head. "Don't get me wrong, I enjoy my career and I'm good at what I do, but that's just a part of my life. It's not all that I am."

"That isn't the message you were sending the other night," she interjected. "The way it sounded when you agreed to help with the congressional investigation, you couldn't wait to get started."

He nodded. "I know that's the way it seemed, but I wasn't taking the job because I couldn't resist the chance to work. I took the job because I felt the need to run."

It felt as if her heart shattered all over again and Melissa wondered how he thought his explanation was better than her assumption. "Y-you didn't have to…go to those lengths to get away from me," she said, hating that she could no longer keep her voice steady. "All you had to do was tell me you'd changed your mind."

"No, Lissa, I wasn't wanting to run from you," he said softly. "I wanted to run from myself."

Confused, she frowned. "I don't understand."

"Let me tell you a story that might help clear things up," he said. She didn't understand how that was going to make his explanation any clearer, but she could see from his expression that he thought it was very relevant. "When my mom and dad got married and he brought her to Rainbow Bend, she told him she loved living there. And who knows? Maybe she did for a while."

"Who wouldn't love living there?" she found herself asking.

"After a few winters of being stuck in the house with no way to get out of the valley for several weeks at a time, my mom found it intolerable." He gave her a sad smile. "You know, I can't remember a night when she was still with us that I didn't lie awake listening to her beg my dad to sell the ranch or, later on, threaten to leave if he didn't."

"Oh, Shane, I'm sorry," Melissa said. "That's why you kept warning me about being snowbound, isn't it?"

He nodded. "I wanted you to know up front what you were getting yourself into."

"Your mother wasn't from around here, was she?" she asked suddenly.

"No, she was from somewhere in Florida," he said, looking puzzled. "But why does that matter?"

"Because she wasn't used to the type of weather we have here." Melissa wasn't excusing the woman's behavior, but she was certain the differences in climates had to have come as quite a shock. "I grew up here. I'm used to deep snows and the difficulties that poses to traveling. She wasn't."

Shane seemed to mull that over a moment before he nodded. "You might be right about that. But it doesn't excuse her from leaving her husband and son and never looking back."

"You never saw her again?"

"No. I was notified a few years ago that she had been killed in a car accident."

Melissa could understand a child not seeing their mother due to death. Her own mother had died of cancer when she was two and she'd known Margaret Jarrod only through the pictures her father had kept. But how could a mother willingly walk away from her child and never contact him again?

"How old were you the last time you saw her?" she asked.

"Nine." He met her gaze head-on, and she could tell that he was still haunted by the abandonment. "But I actually lost two parents that day."

"But I thought your dad didn't pass away until your last year of college," she said, confused.

"His spirit was gone long before that," Shane said, sighing heavily. "After he finally crawled out of the whiskey bottle and burned everything that hinted at a woman ever living in the house, he did two things for the rest of his life. He worked and slept. Beyond that, he didn't have a lot of interest in life."

With sudden clarity Melissa knew exactly why her father had turned into a workaholic. He'd been trying to fill the void left by his wife.

"Did your father leave a picture of her for you?"

Her father hadn't been able to get rid of anything that had belonged to her mother.

"No, I barely remember what she even looked like." Shane shrugged. "But I made a vow that I'd never put myself in the position for the same thing to happen to me. I wasn't going to give that kind of power over me to any woman."

Afraid that his next revelation would be that he could never give her what she needed most—his love—she bit her lower lip to keep it from trembling a moment before she asked, "W-what does that have to do with you helping the senator?"

Shane walked over to kneel in front of her. "I was trying to run from the fact that I'd done the very thing I'd swore never to do, angel."

Melissa closed her eyes and tried not to read anything into what he had just said. She couldn't bear it if it turned out she was wrong.

"What were you trying to run from, Shane?" she finally found the courage to ask.

"I was trying to run from loving you, Lissa," he said, taking her hands in his. "There isn't much of anything in this life that I can honestly say I'm afraid of. But the thought of loving you the way I do and having you leave me one day, scares the living hell out of me."

Tears filled her eyes. "You love me?"

Nodding, he took her into his arms and crushed her to his broad chest. "I love and need you more than I need my next breath."

Before she could tell him that she loved him, too, he covered her mouth with his. Heat streaked throughout her entire body when he traced her lips with his tongue and she readily opened to grant him the access he sought. As he tasted and teased, her heart filled with the knowledge that Shane loved her. She'd never felt more complete than she did at that moment.

When he finally broke the kiss, Melissa leaned back to cup his face with both hands. "Shane Mc-Dermott, I love you with all my heart and soul."

"And I love you, angel." He gave her a quick kiss, then lifted her left hand to slip her engagement ring back onto her finger. "Promise me you won't give this back to me ever again."

Throwing her arms around his neck, she shook her head. "Never." It suddenly occurred to her that he had been wearing nothing but a towel from the moment she walked into the room. "Where did you keep the ring while you were telling me about your parents?"

He laughed. "You didn't notice that I kept my left hand closed?"

"I…well…not really." She smiled. "I was too busy looking at your…um, heart."

"Like that, do you?" he asked, grinning. He took her hand to place it on his chest. "It belongs to you now, Lissa. My heart, my soul, all of me belongs to you for the rest of our lives."

"And I'm yours, Shane," she promised. "I have been from the moment we met."

Lifting her, he sat down and settled her on his lap. "We have a few more things we need to discuss."

"What would that be?" she asked, laying her head on his shoulder.

"I believe you when you say that you love the ranch," he said slowly. "But I think we'll build a house here in Aspen to live in during the snow season."

Sitting up, she frowned. "But I won't mind being snowed in as long as it's with you."

He laughed. "I know, but I'm thinking down the line." He placed his hand on her still-flat stomach. "When our baby is old enough, I don't want to have him or her living with relatives to attend school like I had to do."

"I hadn't thought of that," she said, liking the idea that he wanted them to all be together.

"I also think it would be a good idea for us to spend this winter at Willow Lodge." He kissed her nose. "That way we won't miss any doctor appointments because of weather."

"You're just full of good ideas, aren't you," she said, unable to stop smiling. "That way while you're traveling for the congressional investigation, I'll at least have Erica and Avery over from time to time."

"You can have your family over as much as you like, but I'll be there, too," he said, pressing his cheek to her temple.

"You will?"

Grinning, he nodded. "I called Senator Kurk this afternoon and told him that after careful thought, I wouldn't be available for the job after all."

"Did he understand?" she asked, wondering if he'd made an enemy out of an old family friend.

"He told me he was disappointed, but he understood that being a newlywed I wouldn't want to be away from you." Shane kissed her temple, her cheek and the tip of her nose. "And that brings me to the last thing we need to talk over."

"A wedding date?" she guessed.

He nodded. "Are we still good for New Year's Eve, angel?"

"Absolutely."

He nibbled kisses along the side of her neck. "Why don't I get dressed and you take off the rest of the afternoon. I'd like to take you back to Willow Lodge and catch up on the three days we've been apart."

"That sounds like your best idea yet, Cowboy," she said, loving him more with each passing second.

He was her heart, her soul, her very life. She couldn't wait to be back in his arms again, celebrating the happiness of finding each other, the life they had created and the love she knew for certain they would share for the rest of their lives.

* * * * *

Silhouette® Desire

COMING NEXT MONTH

Available October 12, 2010

REQUEST YOUR FREE BOOKS!

2 FREE NOVELS PLUS 2 FREE GIFTS!

Passionate, Powerful, Provocative!

HARLEQUIN®

A Romance

FOR EVERY MOOD™

Spotlight on

Inspirational

Wholesome romances
that touch the heart and soul.

See the next page
to enjoy a sneak peek from
the Love Inspired® inspirational series.

*See below for a sneak peek at
our inspirational line, Love Inspired®.
Introducing HIS HOLIDAY BRIDE
by bestselling author Jillian Hart*

Autumn Granger gave her horse rein to slide toward the town's new sheriff.

"Hey, there." The man in a brand-new Stetson, black T-shirt, jeans and riding boots held up a hand in greeting. He stepped away from his four-wheel drive with "Sheriff" in black on the doors and waded through the grasses. "I'm new around here."

"I'm Autumn Granger."

"Nice to meet you, Miss Granger. I'm Ford Sherman, from Chicago." He knuckled back his hat, revealing the most handsome face she'd ever seen. Big blue eyes contrasted with his sun-tanned complexion.

"I'm guessing you haven't seen much open land. Out here, you've got to keep an eye on cows or they're going to tear your vehicle apart."

"What?" He whipped around. Sure enough, mammoth black-and-white creatures had started to gnaw on his four-wheel drive. They clustered like a mob, mouths and tongues and teeth bent on destruction. One cow tried to pry the wiper off the windshield, another chewed on the side mirror. Several leaned through the open window, licking the seats.

"Move along, little dogie." He didn't know the first thing about cattle.

The entire herd swiveled their heads to study him curiously. Not a single hoof shifted. The animals soon returned to chewing, licking, digging through his possessions.

Autumn laughed, a warm and wonderful sound. "Thanks,

I needed that." She then pulled a bag from behind her saddle and waved it at the cows. "Look what I have, guys. Cookies."

Cows swung in her direction, and dozens of liquid brown eyes brightened with cookie hopes. As she circled the car, the cattle bounded after her. The earth shook with the force of their powerful hooves.

"Next time, you're on your own, city boy." She tipped her hat. The cowgirl stayed on his mind, the sweetest thing he had ever seen.

Will Ford be able to stick it out in the country
to find out more about Autumn?
Find out in HIS HOLIDAY BRIDE
by bestselling author Jillian Hart,
available in October 2010
only from Love Inspired®.

INTRIGUE

A MURDER MYSTERY LEADS TO A LOT
OF QUESTIONS. WILL THE ANSWERS BE
MORE THAN THIS TOWN CAN HANDLE?

FIND OUT IN THE EXCITING
THRILLER SERIES BY BESTSELLING
HARLEQUIN INTRIGUE AUTHOR

B.J. DANIELS

WHITEHORSE
MONTANA

Winchester Ranch Reloaded

BOOTS AND BULLETS
October 2010

HIGH-CALIBER CHRISTMAS
November 2010

WINCHESTER CHRISTMAS WEDDING
December 2010

HI69501

HARLEQUIN®

American ★ Romance®

Babies & Bachelors USA

Texas Legacies: The McCabes

The McCabes of Texas are back!
5 new stories from popular author

CATHY GILLEN THACKER

The Triplets' First Thanksgiving
(October 2010)

Paige Chamberlain desperately wants to be a mother...
but helping former rival Kurt McCabe raise three
abandoned babies isn't quite what she had in mind.
There's going to be a full house at the McCabe
residence this holiday season!

Also watch for
A Cowboy under the Mistletoe *(December 2010)*

"LOVE, HOME & HAPPINESS"

www.eHarlequin.com

HAR75329